MW01137620

Carolina Down:

A tale of the Average Joe Prepper

By: Jerry Ghent

1.

*"If it's manmade, it **will** fail. Not if, but when."*

"A disaster will happen, it's just a matter of time."

Most people know the first quote and are aware of the possibilities. Their car breaks down only a week after the sale is final. Plumbing problems that flood a basement. Nothing that money and a professional can't help, or some can do attitude.

Most people have heard the second quote as well but ignore it with the mindset that it will never happen to me. Tornados, earthquakes, fires, famine, and landslides are mother nature's test. Pass or fail. Self-pity afterwards or rebuild. People see these on their TV and still they rarely do anything proactive to be prepared.

These don't even include the man-made horrors such as War or power failures on a massive scale. Nations are constantly threatening each other with Nuclear war and annihilation. Nobody wants that because there would be no winners. Just radioactive wastelands. But what about an EMP (electromagnetic pulse)? Or cyber warfare on the power grids? Devastating to the modern civilizations.

2.

Jared Glover had thought about these scenarios' day after day. A prepper for a decade now, he had amassed a decent amount of knowledge and supplies. It was no secret. Family and friends alike knew what he did in his spare time. He even tried to help others get together a simple backup plan in case of any blip in their daily routine. Some took to it, yet others just ridiculed him for it. They always said the same thing,

"If anything happens I'll just come to your house."

He would give the same answer to everyone, *"Come on over but I won't be there. I'll leave the door unlocked so you don't have to kick it in."*

At the age of 39 he had a small house in the town of Lexington, North Carolina, a city of a little over 19,000 residents. He had bought the house before this new lifestyle, so it had absolutely no strategic value or way to "bug in" if necessary. That was something he had never thought about before. One day he'd get a better place, but funds were limited. His days were usually the same...work, work work then see his two kids on his off days. Todd was the average twelve-year-old boy with his video games and Pokémon cards and still had his innocents from the world. Gloria was a few years older at sixteen and just started driving. Both were great kids and understood why their dad did the stuff he did. They really didn't participate unless it meant fire starting or shooting. Just the things they thought were cool. Everything else they just wanted him to do...the typical American kid attitude. Just the Average Joe family.

3.

July 27th, 2019

The United Nations were having troubles as usual with several countries not wanting to play fair and get along with the rest of the world. Hollow threats that fell upon the deaf ears of civilians. More economic sanctions were put in only to be followed with more threats and chants like "***Death to America***". Nothing new. Not much changed. The fire was stoked, and the bear was poked. It happened every year like clockwork...like the Doomsday Clock. It gets closer to midnight then falls back when tensions ease only to get closer to what scientist that created it say is a doomsday scenario. When Jared talked about prepping to someone or mentioned the word Doomsday, he really preferred the acronym TEOTWAWKI (The end of the world as we know it), the other person suggested the zombie apocalypse. TEOTWAWKI is more of your everyday routine getting permanently changed such as your lifestyle from another economic depression or recession. It could mean anything from nuclear war to plague or virus pandemic uprooting you and your loved ones to a power grid down situation. People would die at the rapid rate and the United States would take years to recover. That's what he meant. The world as *you* know it has changed. Although the zombie references were a fun way to get younger people involved. If they could tell you what they would do in that situation, then they had the building block for something that was actually serious such as the New Madrid Fault line. The San Andreas Fault was the famous 750-mile fault line in California that everyone had heard about one time or another in their life time. The New Madrid Fault line was one that not many paid attention to even though it could affect parts of Kentucky, Arkansas, Missouri, and Tennessee if a big earthquake happened there. But if something like the Zombie Apocalypse was how they wanted to get started, then so be it. Jared was entertained, yet happy, to help.

Another mundane Wednesday. After having the past two days off from the swing shift, the night shift begins. Jared rolls into work at the local manufacturing plant. Machinery needed fixing and he was the guy to keep it on track. Just a smooth ten-minute ride from his house he was lucky to have a good job around these areas. Since it was late July the nights were late, and the sun stayed out until 9pm. But he really preferred the winter. If you had to put a coat on to go outside, it was a good day. Or so that was his way of thinking. The Carolina summers of hot and humid never really agreed with him but he was here until his kids could move out and be on their own. Maybe then he would move to another location.

He would hate to leave the "Plan B" crew behind. That was the name of his local prepper group. Eight other men and their families with nearly the same mind track as his when it came to preparedness. They joked around with several names for the crew but would always say when "Plan A" didn't work out (which is life going on normally with no messy disasters) Plan B would kick in...so the name just stuck. "***Plan B, Davidson County Militia***"

For the next twelve hours he would mess around the maintenance shop with side projects until his walkie talkie went off and a production worker needed assistance with a machine. It was a good job and he really couldn't complain too much. When 7am hit and the new crew came in they would sit and chat for a few minutes about work and home life. Then off to the house for a few hours' sleep. It was never really good and kind of hard to sleep during the days even with blackout curtains. The human body just wasn't nocturnal. And that damn kid next door playing the tuba everyday didn't help any either, but Jared was too nice just to go over and crush his dreams and get him to stop practicing.

4.

After getting up, Jared would do so several hours before his shift begins so he could wake up and hit the gym for a little bit beforehand. He had always considered physical training to be a valid and important part of his prepping mind set, this was mainly taken from his days as an Infantryman in the Marine Corps. Sadly only a few of the Plan B crew shared that mind set. Others just wanted to drink beer and shoot guns. And they were damn good at both. Straight shots and that's what mattered. A mix of civilians and veterans evened it out well. They did however train together and knew each other's limitations, but some were in better shape than others. They would regret that decision later.

He kept a close eye on the news even though it was a constant downer. Every single day it was bad news this and guess who's pissed at that. It was more than enough motivation to keep doing what he did. Global superpowers like China, Russia, and The United States were constantly stepping on each other's dicks. If it wasn't trade wars it was disputes over tiny islands or nuclear disarming talks that most said they were doing yet didn't do. Smoke and mirrors. As well as the $22 trillion debt and bloated spending with the ever so present terrorists' threats. Yet only 1% of the 330 million

Americans had a plan in place for emergencies. It honestly blew his mind that so many people just ignored the obvious warning signs of hard times ahead. At times ignorance can be bliss.

5.

Back on day shift he got to work with the day crew fellas. A good group of guys who were hunters and avid political complainers. A lot of the times when something like a natural disaster hit, like the Texas floods or something political like another North Korean missile launch, the conversation would always steer towards Jared's prepping. He had never really told his coworkers what he did, they just eventually figured it out...mainly after he bought the 5-ton military truck and the pages he followed on social media. The pieces just fell in line.

"Hey Jared, guess you'd better go out and get another bag of rice", or someone trying to be slick and gather intel from him by asking how many years he could live off his supplies. He would give the same response,

"That's classified", with a goofy smile.

They could know all they wanted about his lifestyle, he'd be long gone at the first sign of immediate trouble. It didn't affect him any either way. He would joke back whenever someone said they bought their wife a new expensive purse or some useless gadget they didn't really need, "That purse was $200? That could have got you three boxes of MREs or a month of freeze-dried food", or if it was cheaper like a thirty-dollar gizmo he'd say, "That could have got you a can of freeze-dried cheese." Dropping subtle hints that they may want to think about. They'd laugh and wave it off but at least he tried.

You would think they would care with a nuclear power plant just sixty miles south of them near Charlotte, but they would just shrug it off. Their choice. Having a nuclear meltdown for whatever reason was enough for Jared to keep a Geiger counter around. The internet was flooded with this stuff since North Korea and Iran had become nuclear capable countries. It would alert him to ionizing radiation if it did happen. Hopefully, he would have some type of advanced warning like from the radio to keep him updated. That would be enough time to get his stuff and head out during an evacuation. He kept a separate black box with extra gas masks, filters, potassium iodide pills, along with Tyvek coveralls to help keep stuff off the bare skin. It doubled as a biological box as well, so he could use it if a pandemic had started to spread as well.

Again, like every other time and from countless people

he heard, "*I'll just go hunt and fish if I have to and head for the woods.*"

Jared had already done the research, in Davidson county there are 164,622 people. And guess what they all thought? "*I'll just go into the woods or down to the lake for food.*" Some of these people can't even boil an egg without YouTube, let alone go back to pioneer skills. It would be a blood bath of constant mistaken identity. Hungry "hunters" seeing a bush move and blindly fire into it without any positive identification of the target. The human injuries will quickly out do the animal kills. The water illness would be a pandemic all on its own. Backed up waste water plants flooding into the local streams and eventually into High Rock Lake. An enormous manmade lake that thousands of people flocked to every summer to beat the heat. Again, it was their choice. He could give all the warnings and advice until he was blue in the face, yet it still didn't matter. Oh well....it would be their funeral, literally.

6.

Monday, February 3rd, 2020 the warning signs intensified.

The overseas talks had crumbled. Diplomat's with their fancy words and empty promises just wouldn't or couldn't cut it anymore. America had enemies and they wanted us gone, or at the very least crippled and confined to our own shores. But with us being the top military dog on the block, they couldn't just reach out and attack us. We were too strong and technologically advanced. There had to be another way. The news reported that the talks had just stopped. Several countries including Iran, North Korea, China, and several others had pulled back all diplomats from the USA. It was obvious that something was going to happen, yet people said it would all blow over and nothing would happen. They were wrong. Dead wrong. Everyone asked, *"What's the possibility of a 3rd world war?"* or said *"America is too strong to attack directly."*

Jared started to get all his affairs in order and getting his supplies ready and on notice. The 5 ton he named "War Pig" (from a Humvee in Fallujah, Iraq during Operation Phantom Fury) went into full "Bug out" vehicle mode including dropping 4x6 trailer on the back to turn it into a quad cab for extra passenger room. He had to cut out the rear of the cab and side of the trailer to make a small door and connect them together. He also installed AR500 3/8 target plates on the sides and doors to bullet proof it. He installed three 50-watt solar panels on top of the cab for power on the go with a *Goal Zero yeti 400* power storage bank and three extra 12-volt deep cycle RV batteries for extra power storage as well as several other devices like CB radio and air conditioning (something a 50-year-old military vehicle never had). Other options were installed such as flood lights on the cab and several spots lower on the truck to help blind other vehicles. He did throw the canvas troop cover back on after the modifications to keep his supplies dry. Not the best but was better than nothing. If he couldn't haul it, pull it, or push it with this beast, he did not need it. A 6x6 all wheel drive and off-road beast. He believed he had a three-day window if something really bad were to happen. It would take the locals and unprepared a few days to realize help would be strained and hard to get. He didn't want to seem like an alarmist, so he kept his thoughts to himself and left the things in the house where they were for the moment, just better organized and ready to go at a moment's notice. If he was lucky then the governments could reconcile and get back on neutral terms at least.

They did not.

7.

Tuesday, February 19th, 2020

The first of the power surges from the hacker attacks hit the most obvious place...NYC, New York at 5pm eastern standard time. Rush hour. A city that size with the population of 8.5 million people, the panic alone will cause the people to go nuts and start some serious trouble. Local emergency personal will be overwhelmed in a matter of hours. Power transformers surged and exploded in showers of sparks and fires straight down the line from the power stations and into the cities and surrounding areas. Cars crashing from the stop lights blacking out. This was only day one. The confusion will wear off soon enough as they realize this will take a long time and a lot of money to fix and that it's not just a simple "car that had slid into one power pole" ordeals. The real trouble will start as they see the water not running and their bellies start to growl. Civil unrest will closely follow...one of the biggest concerns for a city prepper. They were about to be tested. Hitting this city would be a message that the hackers were more than capable to do more.

No doubt the alphabet agencies such as FBI and CIA would be all over this. They would probably make up some story about a power station worker falling asleep on some buttons. Kind of like the Hawaii missile threat message that was sent out accidentally in 2018 and for 38 minutes people thought a nuclear missile was headed their way and people were panicking, some even shoving their kids into storm drains for an improvised bunker. They would start to fortify the cyber systems in other areas to contain the situation. Probably too late. Hackers and state sponsored cyber terrorist would know the minute they attempted this all other stations would be swamped with government aids to prevent another hit. They would either have planted a virus or continued with more power stations without slowing down.

Washington, DC went black at 7pm. Back-up generators across the city kicked in as transformers exploded and power lines sparked and burned in half creating several fires. It was like a fireworks show gone horribly wrong. This was a direct hit to the central USA government. An embarrassing blow without one bomb dropped. The attack has started, and it would continue. Next, Los Angeles and San Francisco. All happened within several hours of each other. The attack was coming in from all sides. Smaller surrounding cities and towns began to flicker as the power went off and on...then finally off for good. Everything was connected and that was a big flaw. Texan cities were able to fend off the latest attack only because the other cities were going dark first.

8.

Jared watched the news with a blank stare. It was happening. It was no secret that hackers attempted every day, hundreds of times a day, to get into our computer systems. Everything from banks, Emails, and power companies. Report after report had been printed in books and magazines and newspapers. Everyone just assumed Big Brother would keep them out no problem. This is a big mess and was only going to get worse. His cell phone rang as his ex-wife asked what was going on. He explained best he could but no official story from DC had been released yet. Small media stories and explanations were out there but were vague on the details. Witnesses posted shaky videos online as people screamed in the background. The internet was bombarded with all the conspiracy theorist and people wanting answers. He told her to keep the kids at home but make a run for the supermarket for all the last-minute supplies she could get before a panicked society realized what was happening. If there was any trouble at all, just leave.

Too late.

The Wal-Mart parking lot began to fill fast. People had been glued to their TVs much like on 9/11 and had seen all they needed to see. Flustered and scared, they poured into stores across America trying to get what they could. Yet still some people simply thought they were over reacting and just stayed home with what they had already. They were so sure the government would have this crisis taken care of in no time. Little did they know that transformers and power banks took weeks to repair or replace. All new power lines will need to be strung up and installed. And several thousand of them will take even longer. Months even.

The first ones will go straight to the biggest cities for starters to try and reel in the populations there, smaller towns would be last. Sure, government buildings and hospitals had backup generators on hand but usually only a weeks' worth of fuel for them.

Suddenly Winston-Salem, NC went black at 8:42pm. The Eastern connection power grid had been taken down completely. The entire east coast was now blacked out. Parts of Canada were down as the Quebec interconnection that included NYC has been taken down as well. This was a well-organized and well-funded operation that had taken a fast toll on a society so reliant on electricity.

Linda, Jared's ex-wife, had only been in the store for a few minutes before it went dark. People started screaming, pushing, and grabbing for whatever they could get their hands on. Fights broke out whenever two people tried to snatch the same product. She ran and got into her car and went back home empty handed. Before the power went out there, local folks had just watched Four major cities go black. It had gotten too crazy and intense there for her. This reminded her of a picture Jared had sent (one of many) of people on Black Friday fighting over toys and electronics to save a few dollars and it read,

"If they do this over a TV, how will they act when

the food runs out".

She was frightened to her core.

9.

Cell phone towers were now down with no signal getting out to contact loved ones or emergency personal. Jared sat inside his home in complete silence. The darkness was put at bay with the battery powered lanterns he pulled from his homemade faraday cage which comprised of an aluminum trash can lined with foam and a tight fitted lid. It was supposed to be EMP proof and keep his backups safe. Supposedly.

"Whelp, no time like the present to use this stuff", he said aloud to no one. "Time to go. The crowd will be coming soon enough", he realized his unprepared friends and family would now paint him as a target in the weeks to come. They knew he had supplies and they would be out soon enough. No power meant no ATMs, no gas stations pumping fuel to everyone, and soon the water will stop flowing from the gravity fed towers. Jared kept a minimum of ten cases of water on hand at a time for short term water outages like when the city had algae problems and sent out a warning or from a busted water main. Each case had between 28 and 32 bottles in them, so he had nearly 300 bottles to work with before needing his water filters. That would go fast especially with his kids using them. Therefore, he prepped just for dire situations just like this.

At midnight he figured all his neighbors would be asleep and started loading up the back of his truck and the eight-foot trailer that came with it as quickly and quietly as possible, so the neighbors wouldn't know he was taking off. Not until he fired up the War Pig at least, its massive engine kicking to life would ruin the surprise departure. The Cummins diesel engine is the main reason he bought it. It was a multi fuel system meaning it could run on diesel (the best option), kerosene, gasoline with an oil mix, jet fuel, bio diesel, cooking oil, or just plain motor oil he could strain from abandoned vehicles. But it was winter time, so he would need to avoid several of those, so it wouldn't gel inside the fuel lines. The standard tank was 50 gallons and he had another 50-gallon tank mounted for the reserves, both were filled. He always kept them filled for obvious reasons. He really didn't want to leave his home and the unnecessary luxury items like his game systems and air conditioning. Leaving other vehicles behind like his beloved motorcycle would be a bummer but it had to happen. Maybe one day he'll be back for it all, but not soon.

.

Once he loaded up all the food and water and got it situated it had taken up much of what was left of the 14-foot bed (only 10 foot left after the trailer had been dropped on the back). Next came the medical supplies. Everything from dressings, bandages, several bottles of aspirin and Tylenol, to several types of antibiotics, needles, suture kits, and many more items. He had 2 forty-gallon totes filled with medical supplies. Sure, the antibiotics were for made for fish and dogs, but humans could still use them, and they didn't require a prescription. Beggars can't be choosers. He also kept an emergency trauma bag with a small surgical set and IV (intravenous) bags. Basically, if this bag had to be opened, it was a life or death situation. He also kept a small dental kit in a fishing tackle box with instruments and pain medications for crown replacements or cracked teeth. Jared always said he would rather break an arm than suffer any type of tooth pain. The final water proof bin he threw in the back was his small library of self-sufficient books like wild edibles and wilderness skills, he kept the maps up front. He was also glad he had a binder filled with all the useful pages from all the survival magazines he had read. No need to keep the whole magazine, just cut out the pages you needed to cut down on space. These would be worth their time and effort he believed. Speaking of that, he never stocked any gold or silver because in all honestly, if someone was to trade him gold, he wouldn't know if it was real or fake. He never saw the appeal of precious metals. He would always joke around with his crew and say,

"*Dur..look, a shiny piece of metal. I must have it...Dur.*" In his most mocking voice. If he couldn't eat it or use it to catch food or purify water or clean a wound...he didn't want it.

It was now 3am and he was getting tired. He looked at the 8-foot trailer that had been split down the middle. Half was a small cage for the 10 chickens he had and the other half he loaded up with four 55-gallon drum barrels and eight bags of chicken feed. Two were toilet paper, one was laundry soap, and the last one was filled with smaller items such as extra tooth brushes and paste, shampoos, and bar soaps. These would be great for bartering and keeping clean. Sanitation will be a big thing to help keep preventable sickness away. Everyone you talk to that didn't know anything about the prepper lifestyle would always say,

"I don't stock toilet paper. I'll just use a leaf".

Jared would always roll his eyes and respond with, *"Good luck in the winter time when everything is dead and crumbly."*

But again...to each his own. The only thing he had to leave behind was a spare fuel tank that came from an old semi-truck, he kept it fill with 55 gallons of kerosene for his backup heaters. He would use those at night instead of a fire mainly for convenience in the extreme cold or as extreme as it could get in NC to help the central air. He went to the trash cans that the city hasn't picked up yet and pulled them over to the back of the open carport and the rear of the property and covered the tank with all the trash to help conceal it. He threw several other items on top that he didn't think people would be interested in if they came around scavenging. No guarantees but he at least had to try.

That was it he believed. He had put the guns and ammunition on very first thing and spread out into the cab of the truck. The military ammo cans slid perfectly under the seats. It took many years, but he had nearly

12,000 rounds of various calibers, a third of them were
.22s for barter and hunting. It sounds like a lot but will
go pretty fast. It was time to gear up. He threw his bullet
proof carrier vest onto his shoulders that had 6 spare
magazines for his AR-15 (the rifle was sprayed painted
different shades of brown and green to break up the
silhouette) and one in the rifle itself, 2 extra pistol mags
for his 9mm Canik TP9SF pistol in coyote brown, inside
the vest were Scorpion AR500 plates, one in the front
and one in the back. On the back he had his camelbak
water pouch. He snapped on his pistol belt with said
pistol on his left side because he shot pistol left handed
(but rifle right handed, weird he knows), a drop pouch
for spent mags because you didn't just want to throw
them on the ground, an IFAK (individual first aid kit)
and a pouch for his night vision, and finally three
flashbang pouches with two paintball "flashbangs" that
were just bangs and no flash...should have just called
them bangers instead, they inflated and popped in 2
seconds with a CO2 cartridge. Distraction purposes. He
did fill one with cayenne pepper for crowds and people
that just got too close for comfort. The top was reusable
if you could get it back, but the bottom wasn't. That was
ok, he had 10 more spare bottoms. The third flashbang
pouch had a flea and bed bug fogger bomb he could toss
as well. You needed to think outside the box during
times of stress and hard times. It would scatter a crowd if
they saw an unknown canister spraying fog. Finally, he
put on his Kevlar helmet he got from an army surplus
store. Less than a hundred dollars to protect your noodle,
it was a no brainer. Pretty much the same thing he had
been issued during his service time. Of course, newer

and better things were out there but he was on a budget and couldn't get the latest and greatest that Spec Ops guys used. Oh, how he wished he could. He got into the War Pig and sat behind the steering wheel and cranked her up then just stared at his home. He knew it was just a place, but it was *his* place. His comfort zone away from the rest of the world. The diesel engine growled to life and was very noisy. This would make sneaking around a problem. He would have to find a safe location to stash it. He wasn't really worried about someone sneaking up and stealing it. It had three switches that needed to be flipped and were in three different locations just as an extra security precaution. It needed switches for the simple reason all military vehicles didn't require keys. Which made sense because privates were always losing shit. Like the saying goes, "*If you put a private in a room with any item, he'll either break it, lose it, or get it pregnant.*"

Now he must find another place to hunker down. He needed to stay near Lexington to help look after his sister and her kids as well as his mom and her life partner. These were the only ones other than the Plan B crew and his kids he would help and ensure they had at least the bare minimum to survive. In all he had four adults (including himself) and five kids to look after. This would be no easy feat to do. Supplies will dwindle fast as he is the only person in his family to have and extensive plan. His mother Gwen and her life partner Daisy had a few things together. They had just started their backup plans after Jared gave them a "get home" bag and they read the books like "*One second after*" by

William R. Forstchen and the "*Going Home*" series by A. American. The part that really stood out to them were the 9 out of 10 death rates in the first year of a Grid down situation. This is just something they didn't want to go through, mainly to keep their grandchildren from such awful deaths. They only had a few weeks' worth of supplies like food and water, so it would have to do for now. He decided to head to his mother Gwen's house to fill her in on the news and his decision to bug out.

As he pulled up to her house, he had to park in the yard. The paved driveway would crack and split under the 23,000-pound truck. He didn't see either of the vehicles. Then it dawned on him... they worked in Salisbury at the food distribution warehouse for the big chain grocery stores.

"Shit" he thought, "I'll wait here until they come home."

10.

It was 8am Wednesday morning when Gwen pulled into her drive way. She nearly fell out of her truck trying to get to him, eyes red from tears and a scared look on her face. Jared ran up to her asking if she was ok.

"Yea I am. It's just been a long night. It was just so dark... like creepy dark. I didn't want to leave in the middle of the night to come home," She said exhausted.

"From what the radio has been saying, this is a grid down situation. The whole east coast is dark." He didn't want to scare her even more than she was, but it had to be said. "No way to sugar coat it. Sorry."

"I know", tears streamed down her cheeks as she talked "we've been listening to the CBs all night and our truck drivers have been reporting the same things from all over."

Jared looked around and still hasn't spotted Daisy yet.

"Where's Daisy? he asked.

Tears flowed even harder, "She was doing a delivery to Hickory. We raised her on the CB and she said she was stranded in traffic. Crashes everywhere. Blocked roads. That was a few hours ago so I don't know now."

"Ok, let's get inside and go over a few things", he motioned for the front door.

11.

They went through what they knew and what they had on hand. Soon they would need to go to his sister's house to check in and make further plans. They would use Daisy's vehicle when she got there so they would wait a little longer. If she didn't show up soon then they would leave a note and return later. The ball really needed to start to roll, the sooner the better.

An hour had past so Jared decided to leave the ′note. Climbing into Gwen's smaller truck to save on noise and appearance they headed out. He wanted to go incognito, so he wouldn't arise suspicion from the people in his sister's neighborhood. He stripped off his gear and put his pistol in a regular concealable holster, so he could cover it with his shirt. Putting the gear in the middle in between the driver and passenger seats for easy access if needed. He highly doubted it had come to that much hostility already but better safe than sorry.

Jared rode in the passenger seat with his AR-15 below the window as Gwen drove. As they made the drive a few miles down the back roads to his sister Abigail's house, she liked to be called Abby for short, a few cars were on the road. By this time is was nearly noon and the morning frost had started to go away until it would reappear that night. As they passed a trailer park Jared thought to himself, "*Unless they have a kerosene heater back up, it's going to get pretty chilly in those places.*" Life was going to be miserable for the foreseeable future. He wondered what these people would do to survive. How will they act? Do they have any useful skills? He tried to put the thought out of his head. Adding more people will add a strain to his limited resources. They can start a garden in a few months to help out. That will be the best option. Getting people to help out in a trade, labor for food may be an option as well. Then again you would have to worry about them bringing more people over to raid your camp. He would cross that bridge when he came to it. Until then he would have to look out for his own clan first for the time being. Once he got back to the War Pig he would try and radio the group on his portable ham radio. They needed to review their plans.

At the end of a small enclosed round about road that housed thirteen houses, five on the left side and five on the right side with three houses at the end in front of the roundabout, Abby's three-bedroom, two-bathroom house sat as the last house on the left side. The truck came to a slow and steady stop on the gravel driveway. Jared looked around and didn't see much activity. A few kids were in the neighborhood riding bikes and laughing. That's a positive from this ordeal, no more screen time for a bit. He didn't see any of his nieces around. There were three of them. August was the oldest at 15, Sandra who like to be called Sandy was next at 14, and lastly the youngest Vicky, short for Victoria was 11. Jared got out of the truck and walked around to the backyard. The grass had recently been cut. That was a good thing because it will be awhile before people want to waste precious fuel on a tidy yard. Three bikes sat next the back porch and a dog house sat further back. A few toys here and there but nothing major worth noting. He walked back around to the front the see Gwen knocking on the front door. A moment passed before Abby opened it slightly with the chain lock still on. Seeing them was a relief. She quickly closed the door, so she could undo the chain lock to let them in.

Jared made sure the truck was locked before making his way inside for the small reunion. All the girls were sitting in various places and all were covered up in blankets like Eskimos. Since the heat pumps went out and they didn't have a backup heat source, the inside of the house was probably near 50 degrees and even colder at night. He didn't know for sure without a thermometer.

It had to be in the 30s outside at least. It's too cold here for them and they would need to be moved to their mom's house. At least she had a fire place.

Abby filled them in on what she saw on the news before it all went black. Same thing everywhere. It was breaking news, so it was on almost every channel. However, she did tell them something they didn't know which was very interesting. One of her neighbors worked for the Lexington Police Department and all units had been called in for a situation assessment and get ready for a town meeting later in the day. She knew this because she had talk to his wife earlier to see if he had any idea if the power companies were doing anything to fix this. Jared wanted to be there for the meeting to see if any new developments had come in from the state level.

"I'll go to the meeting tonight and see what's going on. Mom, you can go back home and wait for Daisy. I'll set up the CB in my truck and you can monitor it if you want." Jared hoped Daisy would make it back soon. Hickory was an hour away on a normal day.

Gwen agreed that that would be the best idea.

"Abby" Gwen said in a low tone and away from the girl trio, "You need to go through this house and pack some clothes. Y'all need to come and stay at my house until the power comes back on. Mainly because of the cold weather."

Abby was a little hard headed at first but then gave in. It

was the obvious thing to do. The girls would freeze to death if a sudden cold snap came through without any way to warm the place and she only had so many blankets. She agreed the girls and herself would head over to Gwen's house by night fall. It would be cramped but that would be better than the constant shivering here.

Jared and Gwen left after the arrangements were made.

12.

Gwen's truck still had three quarters of a tank of gas, so they decided to make a quick run into town to get an exact time for the meeting and maybe some other useful information. They drove up Main street passed the Sheetz gas station to see the lot full of cars and lines forming for gas. No one seemed to be pumping so they must not have a generator or hand pump at the moment. Jared was sure that wouldn't last long, and someone would provide one...for a fee of gas probably. Passed the gas station about half a mile the local State Troopers office that was attached to the DMV came into view. He pointed to it, "Looks like all hands-on deck and they are all topping off their tanks too." He could see they had their own pumps. Most law enforcement stations did. Probably a good thing.

"They may want to leave a guard on site. People will get desperate." Jared said. He wondered how long they would stick around before abandoning their post to stay with their families. He really couldn't blame them because he would too. They drove past without slowing down. The biscuit place was closed. Made sense.

Another quarter mile down an ATM appear, a few cars and people surrounded it still trying. Wouldn't be long before it will get busted open. People offering any type of anything will want cash only...and probably jack up the prices. More businesses were closed except for the Lexington Farm and Garden store. Gwen pulled in and suggested they see what they can get with the cash she had on hand. They parked and went in. The old man at the counter had made a sign that said, "CASH ONLY, NO CHANGE GIVEN".

They looked around and were the only ones in there other than the employee, or owner, Jared wasn't sure. Then they went to the seeds and filled a bag with various types of fruits and vegetables. This will make all the difference in a few months. They were sure to grab the heirloom seeds and not Genetically Modified seeds because GM fruits and vegetables didn't produce usable seeds for the next year. They were sterile. And who knows how long this will last.

Jared put the bag on the counter and counted 53 bags of seeds.

"That'll be $53 please", the old man stuck his leather-like hands out.

"The price says 25 cents each, that's way less than $53" Gwen said.

"Well today they are one dollar each. Take it or leave it." The old man didn't care whether they bought it or not.

"Fine", Jared handed over the money and they left.

"I have some already, but we'll need more", Jared said as they got into the truck.

They continued up Main Street, it was a straight shot to Center street and turn left to the town hall. This is where the meeting will be. They weren't sure what to expect. As they drove they could see the blown power transformers and power lines that had been fried and laying everywhere on the ground.

"They better get some workers up here to clean this stuff up before tires start going flat." Jared said as Gwen weaved to avoid major debris. "I honestly didn't expect all this."

They made it to the town hall and a crowd had formed already, demanding answers. The police had formed a riot control line to keep the mayor safe. "Uh oh, this doesn't look good," Gwen said trying to find a place to park. Jared threw a small blanket over the gear to keep it hidden.

The crown looked calm for the most part but still shouted and demanded answers. The mayors aid came out with a bullhorn to address the crowd.

"THE MEETING WAS SCHEDULED TO BE HERE AT 6PM. BUT DUE TO SECURITY CONCERNS AND THE INFLUX OF CITIZENS HERE...IT WILL INSTEAD BE MOVED TO THE

AMPHITHEATER. THE MAYOR IS DOING HIS BEST TO GET ANSWERS AND WILL TELL YOU ALL HE KNOWS TONIGHT. THANK YOU FOR YOUR PATIENCE," the aid looked like an unpaid intern. The voice was nervous and shaky. Probably not the best idea to send that kid out when you want the people to have confidence. Maybe all essential personal were too busy trying to get a grip on the new reality.

"Well I guess I'll be back tonight" Jared said. Turning to head back to the truck someone came running over to him. It was one of the Plan B guys and the unofficial leader, James Waters. They shook hands and proceeded to talk.

James started by saying how he knew all this would happen and it's why he had started prepping and it's an "I told you so" time for others.

"From what we've heard the whole east coast and parts of Canada are down," James said kind of excitedly.

"Yea I know that part, as well as parts of California. That's what I've heard on the radio and CB." Jared leaned against the truck. "That's two of the three main power grids."

"The police are way out numbered here. They only have 63 officers, that's including the reserves and school resource officers. This isn't going to be easy. Just look at these people", James swung his arm around at the crowd to emphasize his point. "They seem uneasy."

31

"Well they had better come up with a great plan and hope some don't desert to defend their own homes and families", Jared looked around, most of the crowds had left for the time being until 6pm that is. A few stragglers stayed around and just hung out. Probably trying to see if the officers knew more than they led on. "We need to meet up and get a plan together. Let's all meet at Dylan's tomorrow morning. Spread the word if you would please. Also, if they are interested in the meeting tonight I'll be waiting at the puzzle piece at 5:30pm and to meet there." James agreed and left. He would be able to stop at their houses on the way to his own.

13.

Now that they were headed back home for a few hours it still didn't seem real. But the evidence was right in front of them as they drove away. It was 2 o'clock when they pulled in Gwen's drive way and still no sign of Daisy's vehicle. She parked and got out. She began walking up the walkway when she stopped and froze solid. Jared nearly ran into her as he was fiddling with his gear from the truck.

"What the hell?" he said.

"The note is gone," she pointed to the front door.

Jared quickly geared up and took point in front of his mother. "Go get in the truck until I say it's clear. If you hear gunshots just leave." She ran to the truck and open the door, at that moment Daisy sprinted from the house and straight towards them, He lowered his weapon with a sigh of relief.

Gwen and Daisy embraced each other as couples do.

"Where have you been?" Gwen had tears of joy pouring out.

"I've only been back for an hour I believe. I don't know. My phone died so I don't know what time it is." She released Gwen and turned to Jared. "I'm so glad to see you. I've parked the rig down the road a ways and down an old gravel road." Daisy pulled a cigarette out and lit it drawing in a deep breath and releasing it.

"What do you mean?" Gwen asked, "It was supposed to be delivered."

"I had delivered to two stores already so it's only a third of the way full. But then again after the stuff I heard over the CB, we'll need it, so I skipped the last store. It's all non-perishables so it won't go bad. If this blows over soon then I'll just return it. No harm and no foul."

"How do you know someone won't find it?" Jared asks. "That's a big thing to hide."

"I parked it down near that old creepy mansion everyone swears is haunted. They should steer clear for a bit. Only teenagers trying for a cheap scare and a place to bump uglies go there in the summer time."

"I don't know about that. We'll take the trucks

and go unload it. Someone could have seen you park it. Also get one of those spare drums so we can get the fuel out." Jared was already moving as he continued to talk.

Jared and Daisy pulled both trucks in behind the semi-truck and Daisy got out to open the doors. Once she did she directed Jared to backup as close as he could to the opening. This way they could just toss everything into the rear without much walking. Four full pallets of products were still wrapped in the plastic wrap the packers had wrapped them in. They wouldn't be able to move the pallet, so it would need to be broken down and moved by the arms full. Jared pulled out his Kershaw Blur pocket knife and started cutting the plastic off. The first pallet was kind of a dud, it had cleaning products, air fresheners, plastic bags, trash bags, as well as several other house hold products that wouldn't be a priority to use. They could use some like the bags and disinfectant and they could try and trade the other stuff. The other three pallets were a jackpot. Cereals, oatmeal, a wide variety of canned goods. All had a good shelf life of at least a year during normal times. All preppers knew that expiration dates were more of a recommendation anyways. Now this was what they were hoping for. Daisy didn't know all the details of her cargo because there wasn't a need to usually, just that it went to a grocery store. Three whole pallets could last a small group a few months and it would help out a lot of people short term wise. They would decide what to do with it once they had it all inventoried and organized. It took a little over two hours to get it all on the trucks, so it would all fit including the fuel in the drum. They didn't want to waste gas for another trip or risk someone seeing them leaving with all this and get the rest after they left. They were sure to cover it with tarps to help conceal it for the one-mile trip.

14.

The amphitheater area was packed. Several thousand residents showed up to get some form of reasoning out of this. Who did it? Why did they do it? And how long will it last? All typical and understandable questions.

Jared had ridden with Daisy to the meeting and left Gwen at home to keep an eye on the place. This would be the new normal for a while. Always have security posted. You never know. Davidson county like many other areas has a drug problem. It wasn't so bad that needles were everywhere like San Francisco, but it was a problem. Theft to support the habit went hand in hand. People not having the means to call the police would make it easier for them to try and steal for their next high. As he said he would be, Jared was at the puzzle piece statue at 530pm. The puzzle piece was an art statue that represented Autism awareness and was placed in front of the art gallery. A few crew members strolled up at various times. The ones that could get away from home for an hour or so. All were wrapped in heavy jackets. February was one of the colder months of the winter here. Jared assumed all were armed with a pistol and a few spare magazines. But none would be drawn today, at least he hoped not.

A line of police officers in regular uniforms made a human barricade in front of the stage. Behind them stood the Mayor and his staff moving about and going through papers. Behind the stage a few more officers were stationed in riot gear as a just in case. A few more were moving through the audience to keep a close eye on them and to weed out any trouble makers or instigators. They knew a good majority of the citizens were armed. It was a place that people believed in the 2nd Amendment as well as hunters. They didn't see any long rifles or shotguns just yet. Probably just concealed pistols. It was a little difficult to see everything. Thick jackets to keep the cold off the skin made everyone look bulky. Honestly, there could be anything in this crowd but most of the people here were good, hard working people that didn't want to fight. They just wanted information. The mayor came to the front of the stage with the bullhorn,

"THANK YOU ALL FOR COMING OUT EVEN IN THIS COLD", the voice ripped through the chilly air and over the audience, "AS EVERYONE CAN SEE WE ARE HAVING ELECTRICAL ISSUES. WE ARE NOT SURE WHO IS RESPONSIBLE OR THE EXTENT BUT AT THE MOMENT IT DOESN'T MATTER. LET THE FEDERAL GOVERNMENT DEAL WITH THEM."

He lowered the bullhorn for a moment to comprise himself as some in the crowd yell for revenge, others asked if it was an invasion, and some asked how many places it affected.

"WE WILL BE SENDING A RUNNER TO RALEIGH TO GET MORE INFORMATION. AS OF NOW WE KNOW WHAT EVERYONE ELSE DOES. WE ALL SAW THE SAME NEWS CHANNELS AND I WON'T LIE TO YOU. THIS IS A SITUATION THAT HAS NEVER HAPPENED TO US AS A COUNTRY."

More shouts came from the audience.

"WE CALLED THIS MEETING TO DISCUSS RESOURCES AND WHERE THEY WILL BE GOING UNTIL FURTHER NOTICE. ALL FUEL WILL BE FOR OFFICIAL BUSINESS ONLY SUCH AS THE HOSPITAL GENERATORS AND EMERGENCY PERSONAL. THE MAYORS OFFICE AND MY STAFF WILL USE SOME FOR OUR BACKUPS TO DIRECT RELIEF EFFORTS. NOW WE DO HAVE A CONTINGENCY PLAN. FEMA AND DHS SENT BOOKS AND TRAINING MANUALS JUST FOR SOMETHING LIKE THIS SO WE DO HAVE GUIDELINES TO HELP US. ARE THERE ANY QUESTIONS?"

Hundreds of hands went up. The mayor pointed at a man.

He asked "Will the rest of us get fuel for our needs?"

"NOT AT THIS TIME. WHEN WE GET A BETTER UNDERSTANDING OF THE SITUATION THEN WE MAY RELEASE SOME TO THE PUBLIC."

That fuel part did not sit well with anyone. They wanted

fuel for their personal vehicles and generators and they wanted it now. Like everyone, they felt entitled to everything because most didn't know struggle. They were able to get anything and everything they wanted or needed at any time. This would get worse before it got better. One lady threw a bottle at the stage but was quickly taken down by the police. The tension rose.

"WE WILL MAKE A BULLETIN BOARD AND PLACE IT AT THE SQUARE BY THE CIVIL WAR MONUMENT WITH UPDATES AS WE GET THEM. YOU CAN PLACE QUESTIONS THERE AND WE WILL GET BACK TO THEM. THAT IS ALL FOR NOW."

The mayor decided to cut it short and it was time to go before it got worse. He didn't even get to tell them the other things he wanted to discuss. They were just too upset at the moment. The public would need some time to calm down and register all of this. They wouldn't be happy, but it was necessary. He and his staff took the back way out to avoid any hostilities and for full police protection.

The crew had seen all they wanted to. They were sure there would be civil unrest. It was time to act. They all left and met at Daisy's truck which was several blocks down the road. Parking was a nightmare. They have only seen this type of a crowd when the BBQ festival hits in October.

Jared started, "Ok fellas, things are about to go south and in a hurry. Some people have only dealt with a small power outage for maybe a few days at a time. Looking at the lines and hardware laying in the streets, I'd say it's going to be a bit longer. Weeks or months. And that is if everyone stays calm and helps. Those people were not happy about the fuel comments and this is only day two. I hope everyone here has a reserve on stand-by."

Everyone nodded. They usually kept a hundred or so gallons on hand just in case and for this exact reason or another fuel shortage like when the Gulf of Mexico was hit and shut down several refineries.

"Also keep a close eye out. For those of you with generators you will be a target for theft because they are loud. Keep them chained up. A trick of theirs is simple, they will bring a lawn mower and sit it beside the generator to mimic the sound and just walk off with it. Cleaver actually. So, stay vigilant and stay armed." James added. "They probably will put the grocery stores on lock down for even distribution a.k.a. soup lines. I know I wouldn't want to work there at the moment."

They all chuckled but the reality was real so they all went their separate ways for now.

15.

Abby and the girls had made it to Gwen's by the time Daisy and Jared had gotten back from the meeting. Smoke poured from the chimney something Jared was glad to see. It was time to warm up and get some food in him. He hadn't eaten since this morning when he cracked open an MRE. It wasn't the best because it was low sodium. They came in fourteen meals to a box instead of the normal twelve like in the military versions, plus they were half the price. That's all Jared needed to hear. He had plenty of salt packets, so it wasn't a big deal.

He walked inside and was greeted by the warm air and the sound of people arguing about how bored they were. This was going to be a long TEOTWAWKI if he had to listen to that constantly. He needed a few hours of rest, so he could stay up the rest of the night. It was 9pm and dark outside. The flashlights and lanterns flooded the house. He would talk to everyone tomorrow about that. But he would let it slide this first night.

Waking up at midnight he started to move around with making as little noise as possible. Daisy was still up and standing by the front door looking out. She had a .22 caliber Henry rifle leaning against the wall as Jared had suggested earlier. He made a low call to her, so she wouldn't be startled and reach for the gun. Friendly fire would be a stupid way to die.

"How's it look outside?" He asked.

"I can't see a damn thing." She said, "Dogs barking and that's all I believe. Pretty quiet so far."

"Oh yea, I forgot to let you use these", he reached into a pouch on his pistol belt and pulled out a pair of civilian night vision goggles. PVS-14 style so it only went over one eye. Nowhere near military grade but it would do the job to secure his home and have an advantage over the next guy.

"Where did you get those?" She asked

"eBay. Less than $300. Nothing fancy but it'll work for what we need it to. Plus, I liked the name...Ghost Hunters. People mainly use these for coyote hunting." He also had an infrared laser/flashlight mounted to his helmet for extended sight range. Still less than a hundred yards but it beats the naked eye in the dark. "I'll take it from here." He said as he put on his helmet and mounted the 14's on the rhino mount and slid it over his right eye.

Morning came with no incidents. It was a relief when the sun started to peak over the trees. The darkness brought on a whole different world. In complete dark with little sound, the brain will start to play tricks on you.

When everyone was up and moving about, Gwen had started breakfast. Trying to get rid of the things in the refrigerator. She would can what she could on the propane grill with the pressure canner. It would take some time, but it needed to be done.

"You know what?" Jared asked Gwen as he kept her company while she cooked.

"What?" She asked as she fried up the last of the bacon on the Coleman propane portable camping stove before the fridge lost what last bit of cool air it had.

"People are going to be doing this same thing.

Grilling everything they can treating this like a big BBQ." He sipped on some instant coffee he saved from yesterday's MRE. He had seven of the big store-bought cans but would wait until the MRE coffee is used up before using the good stuff.

"It's best they do that, or all that food will go rotting away and stink. Then what would they do with it? I doubt the trash man will be around this week." She grabbed a cup and motioned for him to fill hers with some of his brew. It was horrible, but she didn't want to waste it.

"Could be worse" He said.

"You mean one of those EMPs from the books we've read?" She knew it was true.

"Yup. I'll be back soon. I need to get together with the crew and see what they think."

16.

"I see no one went to work today. You bunch of lazy bums." James got a good laugh from everyone with that opening joke. "But seriously, we all know what's going on by now with the power grid. Everywhere you look damaged lines are to be seen."

The guys were at Dylan's dinner table with a topographical map of Davidson county spread out. It was a 2 foot by 2-foot map that they had copied from a North Carolina Topographical map book they had purchased from Wal-Mart and had laminated at FED EX. This was a bird's eye view of the territory they would operate in.

"Now" James said "we have about three days before it starts to get really nasty. That's usually how many days' worth of food the average house keeps on hand at any given moment. Food Lion and Aldi's grocery stores have been hit by people that watched the news and seen the four major cities go down. The police were able to get control of the situation and left a few guards at each. So far that's a good thing but they are still outnumbered by 300 to 1 and that's just in the city. That won't last."

Several kids could be heard in the background as Dylan's wife kept them away from the meeting. They really didn't need to hear this at their age. All were under eight years old.

"I hope everyone has a full tank of gas because that's going to be hard to get," Billy said. He was one of the members that liked to stay active, he had no kids and no girlfriend that we knew about. "We may be walking more by time this is all over."

"Speak for yourself," Jared nudged him.

"Yea you lucky shit and your great Craigslist score," Billy nudged back referring to the 5 ton.

"We will also need to have daily radio checks at noon. We all have plenty of rechargeable batteries and can use generators as well as your vehicles to recharge them, so this shouldn't be an issue at the moment." James took control of the meeting like the leader he needed to be at this time. "Also, secure your generators. The thieves will be out to steal them. I know I'm repeating myself about that but it's important. Stay armed with at least a pistol at all times. We don't know how long this will go on or when the city will get resupplied to help the masses."

The meeting concluded and they all went back to their homes. The rest of the day and night came to pass with still no trouble.

17.

Daisy was still on watch when Jared walked outside at dawn.

"I need to make a run to see my kids and how they are doing", Jared told Daisy as he unhooked the trailer from the War Pig.

"I assumed you would want to", she said in an understanding voice. "You sure you want to take that instead of one of ours?"

"Yes. We still haven't unloaded the other stuff yet. We'll do that tonight. I'll be back by noon. I need to see what their set up is and what they have and how long they can shelter in place."

Once the trailer was set up and stabilized he climb into the truck and started flipping the switches. It would take a second for the vehicle to warm up. Besides that, and the noise and the 50-mph speed limit, those where the only down falls he could list for this thing.

Black smoke bellowed from the exhaust in a fit against the cold diesel. It didn't need a heater because the engine put off enough heat to stay comfortable with just a thin jacket on. It could get brutal in the summer time if the windshield didn't push out for a nice breeze. He did throw on his gear this time, full battle rattle, and put his rifle in the rifle mount tucked away beside the driver's seat. He wouldn't need it hopefully and it would be hard to use in this confined space while shifting gears. He put his pistol in a holster that was mounted beneath the steering wheel for quick draw purposes. He had unloaded most of the truck into the spare bedroom earlier and kept some in it to give to Linda once he got there. It was time to roll out.

18.

Leaving the neighborhood, he got several stares and looks from people outside or through their curtains. Not good but unavoidable. He drove down Highway 8 to merge onto I-85 off exit 91. There he would have to stay on until exit 96 and use it to take Highway 64 to Highway 52 and head towards Winston-Salem. Many times, he had made this drive in the comfort of his tiny red car, and once in this beast when the snow and ice had gotten really bad a few years ago. He wished they lived closer to him and further away from a big city. Oh well. The highway wasn't as bad as he had thought. Not many cars out today and only a handful on the side of the road for unknown reason to him. "Just keep driving no matter what" he told himself. "No stops and don't get out for any reason." The massive bumper and shear weight would make it easy to plow through small cars and trucks if needed. Some people would undoubtedly mistake him for the National Guard and try to flag him down. It happened all the time in the past when he was just driving the War Pig around. People waved at him and gave thumbs up, but that was before all the extras he had installed. He made it to their exit almost a half of hour later and continued the back roads until reaching their house.

He took off his helmet and put the pistol back onto his pistol belt and leaving the rifle in the truck. Making sure the doors were locked he walked up and knocked on door. Still keeping the vest on because he needed to get used to it. He would be wearing it a lot and in different vehicles, so he needed to get it adjusted properly and perfectly.

Linda answered the door and he walked in.

"What are you wearing?" she asked.

"Just my normal everyday hero wear. Where's the kiddos?" He asked looking around.

"In their rooms", she pointed and went into the living room and he followed. "I did what you said. The second the lights went out at the store everyone just started yelling and acting like crazed people. Grabbing stuff and just running out of the store. Didn't even try to pay."

"Yea scared people will do that," he sat on the couch.

"You said we would have between three days to a week before it started to get this bad and it's been less than two. What happened?" she was still upset from being caught in the store during it all.

"Well for starters, the news stories didn't help saying possible terrorist attack on every other screen. People just watched the capitol go black. Something they assumed could never happen, then they saw the other major cities go down. And lastly all the keyboard warriors on social media and YouTube had to put their two cents in about all of this. They had several hours to do so before the rest of the system went dark everywhere on the East coast. Now if it had started here and the information couldn't get passed around so fast, people would've thought a car may have wrecked into a substation or something like that. The panic wouldn't have been so severe this fast", he said matter of factly.

"Oh ok, makes sense", she was hesitant but accepted the answer.

"I'm sure the transformers and power lines sparking and going down everywhere didn't help the situation either", he was proud of himself for the explanations. "How are Y'all doing here food and water wise?", he wanted to get down to business.

"With the stuff you gave us and what I had before? Two weeks I'd say", she could tell he wasn't happy about the explanation.

"You may want to think about packing up and going to stay with your mom back in Lexington. It could be a long time before power is completely restored. But you're closer to Winston so it may be a little faster than us. However, safety in numbers," He pointed out.

"I don't know. I'll need to think about it and see what the kids think." She got up and went to get them.

A few minutes later both were out and sitting with him on the couch.

"Dad? Why are you wearing your range gear?" Todd asked.

"Well bud, honestly some things have happened, and I've had to enact on the backup plans I've told you we have. The electricity has gone out all over and it may be awhile before it comes back on." He didn't want to scare them, but he knew they were in for a rough time. Kids these days with no power for everything? It would be like torture to them. He could still charge their tablets and iPod, but they wouldn't have internet for entertainment. "I hoped you down loaded all the fun games, it's all you're going to have for a while."

Todd really didn't grasp the situation entirely. Something like this was unheard to his generation. Not knowing all about the world and chaos it brings, it made

Jared envy the young. Gloria held on to her dads arm tight. This will all be new to her as well. A sophomore in high school all she cared about was electronics, boys, and her beat up car she got for her sixteenth birthday. She asked for a Camaro, but they said absolutely not. She would use this car until she got better at driving then maybe Jared would co-sign for something a little better she could afford on a part time job. I'll be damned if she would get a sports car just to wreck it like so many others before her did.

"So, what do we do now?" She asked softly and staring blankly at the useless TV.

"That's what I here to figure out and make a plan with your mom."

Linda interrupted, "You two shouldn't have to worry about this stuff. This is adult time and adult business."

Todd stands up "I'm nearly a teenager."

"Sit down boy", Jared pulls him back down onto the couch. "Your mom will think about it. I've given her options to weigh. Now I'll stop by your moms' house in two days to see if you've made up your mind. You know my thoughts on it. Keep the windows and doors locked and I would recommend holstering your pistol and keeping it close. People may get desperate. If you do decide to go, pack up both cars with everything you'll need so you won't need to risk the trip back. Fuel will be scarce soon."

He kissed both kids on the cheeks and got up to leave. Getting to the door he could see a few neighbor kids looking at his truck in awe. They thought it was the best thing ever when he drove it in the snow the last time. It was time to go before even more people became interested.

19.

The drive back was uneventful, and he was glad for it. Won't be long until this stretch of highway will have people walking out of the city if something isn't done. He had the CB radio on and listened to traffic mainly from truckers. They were a great source of information especially if they had just got into the area. Fresh news is always welcomed. He did hear a bit of good news. Texas has held its ground so to speak and still has power to most of the state. A few states in the mid-west were said to have power. Excellent he thought. They were on smaller grids so maybe the feds stood a chance. That's where most of the farms were. Maybe things wouldn't be as bad as he thought. They could use trains to move it. That would be the best option to get the most to one area. Now processing was another story. But, that was way above his area of expertise. The one piece of news that stuck out and he needed to inform the others, apparently the truckers that were still able to drive and were connected to their bosses had received word that all trucks carrying any type of food, fuel, or medicine were to report to the closest police station and stay there. That was very interesting. But who knows how accurate this info was.

He had what his family would need. If they stretched it out and was able to get a garden going, he sees his preps lasting nearly a year, that's not including the stuff from the semi. He hoped everyone like rice and beans. They would be eating a lot of those. It was the cheapest and fastest way to get a bulk supply. Using rice as a filler, one can of beef stew would spread to four people. That would help out a lot. Using wild edibles would certainly help as well. He could stand to lose a few pounds any ways.

Once back to Gwen's place he parked the War Pig in front of the trailer just in case he needed to leave in a hurry. The chickens in the back clucked away oblivious to the world. Nothing changed for them. Eat, sleep, and lay an egg. Jared went to the back of the trailer and opened the bin for their feed. It was feeding time and they were letting him know it. He threw a few cup fulls in the pen and shut the door. The hen house had a side door he could reach in a get the eggs out. Both doors had padlocks. Only five eggs today. Looking around he knew he couldn't keep them in there all the time. Getting them into an actual pen on the ground where they could eat grass and bugs would help stretch the feed longer. Then he spotted the trampoline Gwen had for the grand kids. "Perfect" he thought. String up some fence around that and it can easily be moved around the yard for fresh food. As he stood there thinking about a few other projects, Abby and her kids walked outside to get some fresh air.

"Mom said you left to go see Todd and Gloria",

Abby came and stood side him.

He must have been in deep thought, he had to shake his head to start concentrating on the conversation. "Yea, a quick trip to try and get her to come closer. That drive will be getting dangerous here soon enough and I want the kids as close as possible...or at least with a group for better protection."

"Good. So, what are you thinking about?", they watched as her kids were running around and happy to be outside to stretch. It could get boring and claustrophobic constantly being inside with nothing to do. "If you need help with anything, let me know. They'll need to help out around here even if it's just small chores like cleaning."

"Good" He said, "It builds character."

In the distance he heard yelling. A few houses down a man stood on his front porch yelling and pointing into his closed front door which was made of a fancy glass. Not the best idea for a front door Jared thought. Easily kicked in or destroyed with little effort. A woman jerked the door open and proceeded to yell back. This was not a good day for them. Jared wasn't sure what the entire conversation was about, but there was a lot of pointing at the car, so he assumed it was gas related. The woman stopped and looked at Jared and Abby giving them the 'mind your own damn business' look. That was all they needed. Wasn't worth the trouble to keep looking, especially when tempers were flaring.

They turned away and continued their talk about things that needed to get done and projects that weren't a priority but would make life a little more comfortable around the house.

"Should we really be discussing all of this?" she asked. "I mean it can't last forever."

"We don't know how long it's going to last. But I say definitely several months. When I first started prepping I did all kinds of internet searches on a variety of situations. The one that got me really thinking was when I saw *National Geographic's American Blackout.* A power grid down situation. Anyway, when looking into how a hacker attack on us would work the most popular searches were for sending massive amounts of electricity throughout the lines. It would overload the transformers so much they would fry. The forums and pages from reputable sites including the *Department of Energy* said it would take like 5 months a year to replace the big ones I believe. Don't quote me on that. It's been years since I researched it."

"Is that really true?" an unrecognized voice came from behind startling them both.

"What the shit?" Abby yelped out in surprise.

"Is that true? What you just described?" The man was the one from yelling match they witnessed a few minutes ago.

"I hate to admit it but from all the evidence, news

reports when it started, and blown transformers everywhere. I'm going to say yes, it is." Jared turned fully towards the man. He was a younger white man. Looked to be in his mid-twenties, belly sticking over his belt like most people these days with a shaved head and not that tall which made it worse. Jared was looking for any signs of a weapon but only saw a pocket knife shape in the front right pocket.

"What are we going to do?" he looked shocked and for good reason.

"WE ain't going to anything. And you shouldn't sneak up on people" Abby laid into him for scaring her.

"I know, and I am sorry" he said raising his hands up, palms out like when you want to end an uncomfortable conversation. "My name is John Shield. I live a few houses over. I saw Y'all watching and I needed to get away from that woman for a bit. Figured I come explain it as a non-domestic ordeal just in case someone called the police."

Jared raised his eye brows in the 'you can't be serious' way.

John continued "I see now that that's not going to happen." He looks around and sees the 5-ton truck sitting in the far back of the yard. That was all they could do to keep it from being seen from the road. But the neighbors could easily see it. Nothing he could do about that part. "Nice truck. I've seen it here a few times. Never saw it up close though. You mind?"

Jared really didn't want him to, but it was better than him trying to do it himself at night just out of curiosity. He shot Abby a look like 'crap this sucks' as they all walked over to the massive piece of metal. John looked closely at the doors and wanted to get in it, but Jared said no.

"Fair enough" he said and continued to walk towards the rear. He spotted the chickens in the trailer and scurried to see them. "That's a hand full of chickens you've got. Good to know...good to know."

Jared did not like that response.

"Maybe you can spare some eggs for us later."

"If I have any leftover I might be able to. No promises though." Jared wanted to joke around with it and not get a serious tone. That could rub the man the wrong way and cause unwanted drama. Ah hell, who was he kidding? Drama will start as soon as the other folks around hear about it.

"Guess I'd better go home to see if she's calmed down any. She pissed because we're nearly out of gas." They shook hands and he walked back home.

Jared turned to Abby and said in a low voice, "He'll be back one night. I guarantee."

20.

Noon came, and the radio checks followed as they all planned. Everyone was good. The code phrases from the small hand sized notebooks they all kept were

55

used. Anyone with a ham radio or CB radio could listen in, depending on which one they were using at the time. Code phrases, words, and names had to be used as a primitive type of encryption. None of them could afford those military grade radios that did it for them, so this was the next best thing they decided on. Jared did let them know he may or may not have trouble with the neighbor. The ham radios were a great asset only because of the solar powered repeater the local radio club had installed. They had taken a few classes several years ago with them to get to know the comms better and are glad they did. They weren't official members but were able to bribe one of the members with a new golf club to let them use the repeater and give them the frequency. It was a good trade off that would prove invaluable in the times to come. Technically, you needed certification to use one but in serious situations, does anyone actually care? Nope.

Their code names stayed with the phonetic alphabet used by the military to make it simple and you didn't have long drug out names like "blood agent" or something else stupid.

Jared Glover was Golf

James Waters the leader was Whiskey

Dylan Lackie was Lima

Billy Henderson was Hotel

Dwayne Cruz was Charlie

Martin Gordon was Mike

John Ocwen was Oscar

Pete Coonts was Papa

Anyone whose name started with J didn't wanted to be Juliet. Understandable.

After the radio check with the crew Jared knew he needed to put up some perimeter defense for when the neighbors attempted to get into his chicken coop. Some kind of loud alarm that would scare the crap out of whomever tried to get near it. Then he remembered the mouse trap trick and set to work. He grabbed a small wooden mouse trap from his moms' junk drawer and a 20-gauge shotgun shell and cut the lead projectile out. It was time to make a non-lethal but very loud trip wire. Simple to make and only three parts to it. He cut a hole in the middle of the trap where the metal wire would impact. The wire would be bent downward into a small point, so it would strike the primer when triggered. The hole is just the right size, so the back lip of the shell keeps it from sliding all the way through and sit snug and flush. This would be enough to make anyone jump and run when it goes off, especially in the dark. He could only make four of them total, that's all that came in the pack. He would add it to the list of things that would be useful and start asking around for some. He would place them tonight when it was his turn to stand watch.

To save on batteries and lamp oil the adults decided to make bedtime an hour after dark. The nights would get shorter the closer summer got but for now this needed to happen. Once the kids were settled down and Gwen started her watch at the front door, Jared, Daisy and Abby went to the trucks to unload the big rig score from a few days ago. All the nonfood items went into the building and the food went into the house. Where ever they could find a spot. They could organize it better tomorrow, but tonight they just needed to get it inside before anyone saw them.

21.

The next morning, they all began to sort everything out and organize it with an inventory sheet. It was a decent amount to add to the preps.

"Today I'm going to need a ride to my house. I want to pick up my car, so I don't have to keep using the trucks. Plus, it's better on gas." Jared said as he moved three cases of canned ravioli to one side of the pile.

"Ok" was all Gwen said. They would wait until after the noon radio checks just in case they ran into any trouble getting back.

Noon came, and the radio came to life.

"All stations, all stations this is Whiskey, radio check over"

"Golf check, over"

"Lima checking in, over"

"Hotel compound here, over"

"Charlies in the trees, over" referring to the Vietnam war enemy. They couldn't be serious all the time.

"Mike check, over"

"Oscar here, over"

"Papa here, over"

Everyone checked in with no issues at their homesteads to report. Always good to know.

"This is Golf. I'll be heading to town in a hot minute to see if anything new is going on. Meet at the usual spot if anyone wants to go."

A hot minute to them meant One hour and the usual spot was the puzzle piece.

Everyone confirmed, and he turned his radio off and got a ride to his house. He walked in the freezing cold house. No heat from the air unit or a fire made it just like he was standing outside. Nothing broken into yet, but it was just the beginning and people still had a few resources without burglarizing yet. Daisy left him there and headed back home. Jared wanted to look around just to see if he missed any of the prepper gear or family pictures, everything else he didn't care about. The big screen tv was useless, it would be a waste to power anything bigger than a small portable DVD player. He really didn't see much that he wanted then a knock came on his front door. Putting his hand on his pistol he peaked through the window adjacent to it. It was his neighbor Randy, a retired airplane mechanic from across the street so he removed his hand and opened the door.

"Hey Randy, to what do I owe the pleasure of this visit?" Jared stepped out onto the porch and closed the door.

"Jared, I haven't seen you around in a few days and your big truck is gone. Thought you left town until I saw that truck drop you off. Just wanted to check in on you is all." The old man in his late seventies was always out and about on his golf cart. Not a care in the world. Just drove around the area several times a day. Kind of an impromptu neighborhood watch. No one asked him to do it, but he always said he rather do this than stay inside and rot.

"Yeah, just been staying at some families houses. They have a better fire place and it's easier to keep it lit with more people."

Randy gave him an understanding wave of the hand, "What brings you back here?"

"Just getting my car and I'll be on my way. I won't be back for quite some time. I'll leave the door unlocked so you can walk in if you need anything." Jared wanted to leave. It was getting closer to the meeting time.

"It's quiet around here without the power on."

The old man looked around unconcerned. In his life he had seen several power outages and was convinced it would be back on any day now like it always had in the past. He was in for a shocker later.

"I think it's going to stay like this for a while" Jared said.

"Nah, the government will get it back on in no time." Randy said confidently.

"Take care Randy. I've got to go. Stay warm." With that Jared went around the house and to the car port where his Honda Accord sat waiting on him. He had put the spare gas cans that equaled fifty gallons in the trunk before he left the first time, so his car smelt strongly of the increasingly rare resource. He would have to ride with the windows down in the cold air, so it could air out a bit. At least he has his thick Carhartt jacket on. He cranked the reliable car up and went on with his business.

22.

Across town at the puzzle piece James and Billy were waiting patiently when he pulled up. "Good to see I've got some backup", Jared rolled all the windows up. The breeze took some of the smell away but most clung to the fabric. Oh well. It would have to air out more at Gwen's house. They walked the next three blocks which was a slight incline to their first stop. They wanted to see what the town bulletin board was all about. Getting to the square a few dozen people had gathered. Apparently,

61

they did updates at 6pm. They would get to see yesterday's news unless they waited another five hours for the next. People were moving about, some left and some wanted to ask the two police officers standing there questions they obviously didn't know the answers to. This aggravated a few people just because of shear impatience.

"When will the gas station be open?" or "When can I go shopping again?"

And comments such as,

"I bet they stored all kinds of stuff in the mayor's office instead of passing it out." and "I bet these guys get whatever they want when they want it."

The crew stood in the back and just wanted to listen. They were there to gather intel about whatever they could. The two cops were professionals and answered whatever they could...which wasn't much. The crew moved in closer, so they could read the board. A few announcements were posted. The runner had come back from Raleigh, the state capitol. He wasn't the only runner there. Cities all over sent people to get some information. The capital, after the first twenty or so showed up, decided they needed to print out copies of the knowledge they had and pass out more of the books FEMA had sent years before. The letter was short and all it did was reveal that the Federal government had confirmed the USA was under a cyber-attack and that all National Guard troops would be activated and were to report to their units.

"How are they going to contact all the people to their units?" Jared thought out loud. One of the cops heard him and replied, "The mayor has sent a few units to the Guard Armory on West 9th Avenue to get the list of the Guardsmen addresses so we can send units to bring them back to armory."

"Smart" James said. "Ok, it sounds like reinforcements will be here soon enough." They heard all they needed to hear now. So, they started walking back towards the vehicles. A block away from the cars they saw a man standing behind Jared's accord trying to pry open the trunk with a crowbar. The person didn't even try to be sneaky about it. Just beating, stabbing, and prying. Doing whatever he could to get inside.

"Billy, you circle around the back of these buildings to cut him off. James, you do the same on the other side of the street. Move!" Jared wanted to get to him before he popped it open and saw the gas. All three started to run, they were half way there when the trunk popped open and the guy yelled in excitement. He picked up two of the five-gallon NATO style gas cans and shut the trunk closed. As he did Jared was getting closer, the thief spotted him and started to run. He couldn't go very fast, but he attempted and just kept running south on Main street with the cans in hand. He turned right down the next street and met with Brandon standing there a little winded but gun in view. The man hit the brakes hard and tumbled over with the extra weight. Luckily the NATO cans sealed completely and didn't spill everywhere. Billy snatched him up just as

Jared got to them. A middle-aged white man with blood coming from his upper lip. Looks like he got it in the spill.

"Where's James?" Billy asked as the man struggled to get free. Jared looked around to see James doing a fast walk around the corner of the last building and gasping for air. Jared turned back around, "I'm sure he'll be fine." They both laughed. He picked up the cans and moved them a few feet behind him. Now giving his full attention to the man,

"What the hell were you doing breaking into my car?"

"Come on man, I could smell the gas coming from it. I need it. The gas stations haven't been open in days," The man struggled more but Billy's grip was stronger.

"That doesn't give you the right to steal from me." Jared poked him in the forehead.

"I left you the other cans, man."

They didn't notice the car at the end of the street the man was running towards. It started up and headed their way. James finally made it to them still gasping for oxygen. The car sped up as it got closer, a man leaned out of the rear driver side window and opened fire with a pistol. The bullets flew wildly. It was meant more to scare them and release their comrade than to kill them. Billy let go and dove to the ground pulling his Glock 9mm, Jared dropped to one knee to make himself a smaller target and pulled his Canik 9mm, James fell to the ground pulling his Glock G21 gen 4 chambered in .45. They all took aim at the car and fired as it slowed down just enough for the man to run and dive into the passenger side door then sped off. A few hits were visible in the doors and windshield, but it did no good. The driver wasn't hit, and they got away. The crew stood up, adrenaline coursing throughout their veins. Hearts pumping and sweat flowing.

"Everyone ok?" Jared did a quick hand run over his body to check for blood. Nothing. He looked over to see the others doing the same. They both gave a thumbs up. Best news today. No doubt the police up the road heard all of that, so they waited for sirens. They waited for fifteen minutes and nothing happened. With the adrenaline depleted from their systems they were tired of waiting. Jared grabbed the gas cans and started towards his car.

"What are you doing?" Billy asked.

"I'm leaving" Jared said over his shoulders, "I'm going to put these up then drive up to the police station to see what we have to do."

James and Billy followed. They all got into their cars and decided to drive the five blocks up to the police station, so they could always be watched from now on. The police station was two blocks past the square where the board was posted, at the intersection of North Main street and West 2nd street. They took it slow because all the stop lights were out, and they really didn't need to get into a wreck. Parking in front station James and Jared went inside as Billy stayed behind on vehicle watch. They didn't like it, but they did have to leave their weapons in the cars. There were several citizens inside the building. The lights were dimmer than normal, must be cutting back on the generator to save fuel. They had to wait in line for a few minutes. Finally, at the front,

"I'd like to report a self-defense shooting," Jared told the police woman sitting behind the bullet proof glass. Her hair was all out of place and she seemed stressed.

She sighed loudly, "Was anyone killed or wounded needing medical attention?"

"No, we caught a guy breaking into my car and chased him. His buddies did a drive by shooting on us and we had to return fire." Jared talked steady for someone in his position "Did you not hear it? It was just down the road at the art museum."

"We have had thirteen shootings today, sir. And that's just the ones reported. If no one was hurt and you still want to fill out a report, you can. But as of right now that will not take priority because no one is dead or dying. We'll put it on the list, but we are stretched thin and getting thinner. It could take a while to process it. Once the national Guard gets here we can do it better." She sounded like she had said this one too many times today.

"I'll pass but thanks any ways", and he walked out with James following closely.

"That was fast" Billy exclaimed. "Figured it take a few hours at least."

"They don't have the man power to spare at the moment and no one was hurt so they really don't care now. There are other shootings that have priority." Jared told him.

"Let's go back and collect our brass for reloading", James nodded down the road. "We know now that we cannot rely on the police as backup. This is a learning point that should be taken seriously."

They all agreed and went back to area to collect their spent brass.

23.

Meanwhile in Raleigh, the governor was in a panic over the news he had just received from several runners that made it to him this morning. He sent them back with satellite phones to make communications faster. Only six were available for the moment, so he sent five back and kept one. Also telling the runners to stop in every city on their way home and give the mayors his number and said to try and find a satellite phone as well. There are twenty-two power stations in North Carolina, four of which are Nuclear. Nine power stations across the state had been targeted and destroyed after the power surges. Small groups of individuals had hit the stations almost immediately after the cyber attack and targeted the Computer service rooms and main transformers on the property. These were the two absolute critical and most valuable pieces to the station. Getting these up and running again could take easily up to a year and possibly two years just to build one. He had the printed version of a PDF file that was printed after the last hurricane season had knocked out power for a full week on the coast. It was the *U.S. Department of Energy: Infrastructure Security and Energy Restoration: Office of Electricity Delivery and Energy Reliability.* He's glad he had it printed off instead of just down loaded. He couldn't just do a simple internet search and find this information anymore. He was in his office looking through the book, his aids standing around going through papers and talking into walkie talkies trying to get the state some relief.

"Page 9, ok here it is. Everyone quiet down please." The room went silent as he read aloud. "*In 2010, the average lead time between a customer's LPT order and the date of delivery ranged from five to 12 months for domestic producers and six to sixteen months for producers outside the United States. However, this lead time could extend beyond 20 months and up to five years in extreme cases if the manufacturer has difficulties obtaining any key inputs, such as bushings and other key raw materials, or if considerable new engineering is needed.*"

He closed the booklet and tossed it onto his desk in complete shock and sat down.

After several minutes some finally broke the tension, "What does LPT stand for?"

Another person spoke up, "Large power transformers. Which is exactly what we need...and now."

Someone in the back asked the obvious "So we have at least a year of this mess?"

"Why hit North Carolina this hard? They got D.C. and New York. Why us?" The panicked voices wanted answers. They were scared and they all knew it.

"Because" Looking at a map of NC the LT. Governor said "We have huge military bases here that rely on civilian power stations. Camp Lejeune, Marine Air Station at Cherry Point, Fort Bragg, and Seymour Johnson Air Force base. Also, the Coast Guards Base Support Unit.

"Yes, that would be my best guess" the Governor scooted up to his desk. He had a satellite phone and tried to reach D.C. to let them know the following power stations have been destroyed. He was sure the bases had already reported or attempted to report, but it was also his responsibility as well.

The four top concerns:

- Butler-Warner Generation Plant that supplied Fort Bragg

- Jones-Onslow Electric Membership corporation and the close by Solar Power field near Camp Lejeune

- Duke Energy's H.F. Lee Plant that feeds Johnson Air Force Base

- Duke Energy's Roxboro Plant

The five smaller ones:

- Buck Steam Station in Salisbury (15 miles from Lexington)

- Siemens Power station near Winston-Salem

- Duke Energy Asheville plant

- Marshall Steam Station

- Allen Plant Steam Station near Charlotte

"I understand the ones near the bases but why all of these random ones?" one of the staff members asked.

"In all honesty, who knows how long this has been planned for. Maybe they were the least secure and the easiest to infiltrate. So far there are no reports of the Nuclear Stations going down. They have much tighter security. Cause mass panic of the citizens...who knows. But we are under attack. That much is obvious. This was very well coordinated."

At that moment the call went through and he gave his report to whomever was on the other side. He was told it was happening in several states and the numbers continue to rise.

He ended the call and looked at his staff, "I declare a State of Emergency."

24.

One week after the grid went down, less cars were on the road. Less people were out and even less were friendly. The news of the power station bombings had been posted on the town board two days ago and it made people go a little bit wilder than they would normally. It was a dire situation that nearly everyone wasn't prepared for. First, the power goes out and transformers were over loaded. People thought it would be fixed in a few days, then the terrorist attacks on American soil destroying something that would take a long time to repair. They had all seen the news and what happened to DC, NYC, and LA before the electricity went out. They just assumed it wouldn't get so close to them.

The grill outs that were going on to get rid of the refrigerated foods had stopped. People didn't want to share what little they had anymore. Now they were living off canned goods and box suppers if they were able to cook them somehow. This town needed to come together, or it would be hell to pay. Most of the National Guardsmen had showed up after the police were able to get a hold of them. A few didn't. They could've been stuck out of town or just didn't want to leave their families. 132 troops were now at the armory and setting up for the long haul from there. The mayor ordered all groceries stores in Lexington to be emptied out and all contents moved into the Super Wal-Mart. Three Food Lion stores, an Aldi's, Save-a-lot groceries, a Lidl, and the Compare foods store were emptied and relocated. Wal-Mart was the biggest building to do this and it was easier to guard one place than eight. A few attempts were made to rob the stores but were fended off with a few casualties on both sides. They just weren't used being told when, where, and how much they could get. There would now be rationing. The five pharmacies were emptied as well and moved into the pharmacy inside of Wal-Mart. The last thing the city needed was a bunch of druggies using the much needed and rare pain killers just to get high.

Thirty Guardsmen and a few police officers were always to be on watch. Pathways were erected to keep people in line so there wouldn't be a black Friday type of incidence. Pushing and trampling others just so you could get something first. People were hungry and hungry people became desperate and violent. For the total population, the stores would be emptied in less than a week. It was just too many mouths to feed and in the time of constant resupplies and just in time deliveries had made it unsustainable for any type of long-term situation. Modern civilization had screwed themselves into a hard place of comfort, fast services and products. This would the downfall of American towns if they couldn't come together during this time. More and more break-ins were being reported, some were fended off or the perpetrators were killed, some were bloody, and homeowners lost their lives. Without computers to help identify DNA samples and fingerprints, the authorities could only make reports and save evidence and put them on the back burner until the power came back on.

Police patrol cars were rarely being used, they were using the bicycles that they used during the summer times and for outdoor events. Fuel needed to be rationed and the hospitals were draining the most. They had a few people on life support, a few new mothers, and the emergency room constantly stayed full. Surgeries for gunshot wounds increased dramatically. They had scaled back all the unnecessary rooms, it did help but the massive generators still used a lot. The two ABC stores (alcohol beverage centers a.k.a. liquor stores) had been ransacked and completely emptied. That wasn't a priority for the police to guard constantly. Without power the alarms didn't work so it was free range for all those who wanted booze. And who wouldn't want a stiff drink at a time like this?

25.

Jared went to drop off a few things at Linda's mothers house. Her, Todd, and Gloria had come into town four days ago and were staying with her. They inventoried everything they had on hand. Nobody needed any live sustaining medications so that was a huge plus that would make life less stressful. He had been informed that a lady down the street had died because her oxygen tank had run out. Her body just gave out under the burden of unassisted breathing. A sad note but it won't be the last. In the next few weeks a medical die-off would happen. The folks that had no one to care for them and couldn't get more medications wouldn't last much longer. There was only so much insulin for diabetics and that had to be kept refrigerated. He would be by every few days to check on them and make sure they were safe. Gloria was a crack shot and had been ever since she eight years old. Jared left one of his AR-15s with her. She could load the magazines, break it down to clean it, and before she ever even touched a weapon growing up he drilled the five weapons safety rules into her and made sure she knew how to implement them. He was confident that she could handle herself. Todd knew the same, but his age made it difficult for Jared to let him handle a weapon 24/7 so he didn't leave anything for him.

26.

Noon came around on the ninth day and radio checks still happened. Nothing new to report. It felt like the calm before the storm.

27.

On day fourteen the grocery store stock had run dry. Everything had been passed out and used up. The store was now useless, so the mayor had all the medical supplies loaded up and headed towards the hospital. The thirty guardsmen and ten cops loaded up all the medical supplies in several armored Humvees and civilian box trucks. Taking the lead was the sheriff department's own APC (armored personal carrier) painted all black. It had never been pulled out except for showing it off in the local parades and on big toy day where everyone brought in their hobby vehicles to show off once a year. It hadn't seen action here yet. It was given to them by the defense department like so many other police departments when the wars overseas were winding down and all the older excess and worn out gear and vehicles were returning. Some new paint and a few new parts then it was ready for service. It took the lead with two armored vehicles behind it, six good sized U-HAUL moving trucks, and two armored vehicles in the rear. An impressive display of security. Only and idiot would target this convoy for pills to get high...or so they thought. The price for narcotics and medical supplies was very high. Worth almost anything in trade value, including payments for thugs doing the dirty work.

The trip was only a few miles long to get to the destination. Leaving the front of Wal-Mart and heading north down Cotton Grove road. A mile down the road at the Y intersection where it splits to South Talbert Blvd., once the convoy was in sight and a hundred yards away, several cars that blocked the continued path on Cotton erupted into a fire ball. The convoy skidded to a halt.

"We have a road blockade" The commander of the sheriff's APC said into his radio.

"Push thro..."

The First Sergeant (1SG) was cut off as a semi-truck with an attached trailer came from the left at Guildford street and impacted the first armored Humvee he was in and pushing it into the brick wall on the other side of the sidewalk. Another semi-truck with a trailer attached barrel from the right side out from Oak avenue a hundred yards back and impacting the last armored Humvee. They were now cut off and biggest and toughest of the vehicles was on the other side of the fight. Small arms fire rained down from the roof tops of the local businesses and the alley ways. They would have to fight for their lives to get out of there. The troops returned fire to suppress the once fellow Americans now turned combatants. The rear Humvee that was impacted was now on fire with the doors pinned shut between the truck and a building. The screams from the four men burning alive could be heard all the way to the front of the convoy. It was time to move and move fast. As the troops engaged the enemies, a PFC ran to the front semi-truck and jumped onto the passenger side step. A masked man was knocked out cold behind the steering wheel. He opens the door and slid in, opening the driver's door he pushed the man out and he smacked the pavement head first. Blood gushed from his head with no sympathy from the young soldier. He cranked it up putting it in reverse to move it off the road and un pin the front Humvee where the middle-aged military man was pinned in. Once the truck was moved enough the door flung open as the determined and battle hardened 1SG got out. He opened the rear door to let the other three soldiers out to join the fight. He ordered the semi to back completely off the road, so the convoy can pass. Two masked men emerged from behind the semi-truck firing wildly, the four newly freed soldiers cut them down with ease. 1SG looked at the totaled Humvee and realized it was no good to drive. The obstacle was now out of the way. He yelled into his radio,

"LOAD UP AND LET'S MOVE!"

The soldiers with the mounted machine guns continued to fire as the rest got into the other vehicles for extraction. The three from the damaged Humvee ran and got into the sheriffs' APC. 1SG ran to the rear to assess the burning military Humvee. It was completely engulfed in flames; the front of the semi had caught fire as well. There was no helping those poor souls. They had to be left for collection later. He wanted to tear up but now was not the time. The mission was not complete. It would have to wait. Cramming inside the now last Humvee in the convoy,

"ALL TROOPS ACCOUNTED FOR?" he demanded the answer. He wouldn't leave anyone behind if he could help it. Especially not on accident from a miscount.

All troops rogered up. Time to leave.

"GET US OUT OF HERE, NOW!!!!"

The convoy speed off and continued to their destination. Once there the casualties were listed. Four KIA and two non-life-threatening gunshot wounds.

28.

It was night time and Jared was on watch. His watch said it was 2 a.m. and he was bored out of his mind. He would use his night vision IR flashlight to look around the area. He moved from the back door to the front door, so he could keep an eye out on the whole property. He had set the mouse trap trip wires in several places. One was on the egg door for the chickens, another one was on the people door of the chicken coop, one was placed on the outside buildings' door, and the final one was on the back gate. They were mounted as discretely as possible on one side of the doors with fishing string on the trap release and connected to the wall bracket. When someone opened the door more than five inches without disarming it first...bang.

BANG!!

Jared ran to the back door and peered out. He saw someone running from the chicken coop through his night vision and towards the neighbor's house. The same one that asked for eggs a few weeks ago but never came back. He was trying to steal them. The nerve of that guy. It was time to settle this. The police wouldn't come out of the city limits and the sheriff's deputies only operated in the day time now. They were too busy protecting key city personal and places like the hospital and government buildings that were still operational. He woke up Daisy and told her what happened.

"Take watch. I'm going to have a little chat with him."

He waited for her to get up and wake up for a few minutes. She grabbed her Henry rifle and went to the back porch.

Jared walked outside in full gear. He didn't know

what type of weapons the man had so he didn't want to risk going over there without it. He disarmed the gate simply by easing down the hammer, that was the technical term for the metal part that crushed the mouse. He turned around and replaced it just in case this was a trap to get him out of the house so others could rush in unnoticed. Rifle up and at the ready, he eased across the yards sweeping from side to side looking for threats. None yet. The house was just two doors down, so it would not take long to get there. A faint glow could be seen from a crack in the curtains, probably a candle by the looks of the soft glow. He sped up and got close to the house. The porch was only four steps that turned into a 4x4 concrete slab. Good and sturdy. Once up the steps as quietly as possible, standing beside the door, never in front of a door so they could shoot you through it. He knocked, not soft but not pounding in an aggressive manner. Muffled sounds came from inside like people moving around and trying to whisper. He knocked again and heard,

"Who is it and what do you want?" The man sounded like such a dick.

"I saw you trying to get into my belongings" Jared said with a stern voice.

"Wasn't me" John Shield responded.

"The person I saw running into your front door wasn't you?"

"Sure wasn't" John continued to lie.

"Why don't you come out here and let's have a chat like normal people, Face to face." Jared looked around so he wouldn't be ambushed by someone coming from the rear of the house.

"Nah, I'm good. Just want to go back to bed. You woke us up with your knocking." John didn't dare open the door.

"Ok. But I'll say this to whomever ran into your house after my alarm went off...no more warnings. Shot on sight. Have a good night." He started to walk away when the door flung open and his wife marched out in her night gown and a jacket.

"Who the hell do you think you are threatening us like that?!" she demanded.

"Just someone confronting a thief" Jared said nonchalantly.

"Maybe you should share what you have then we wouldn't have to sneak around" She crossed her arms. "No one man needs ten chickens to himself. Give us a few."

"Um...no." He turned to walk away and heard the metallic sound of a round being chambered into a gun. He quickly spun around and aimed at the woman. She had it in her coat pocket, but Jared didn't notice it with her arms crossed.

"Don't do this" He said.

"Put the gun down Maggie", John urged her.

"No. We are over here starving with little to nothing and he has all that stuff. I know what you are." She kept the pistol pointed at his chest. "You're one of those crazy end of the world lifestyle people the news did a special on last year. You spent all day every day getting ready for stuff like this to happen, so you can be a big shot when it actually does."

"Maybe you should have paid more attention to that show and started putting something back." He kept his aim on her. "Your suffering and lack of supplies is your own damn fault."

"Now now everyone. Let's just keep calm and talk all of this out. No need to get hurt." John tried to be the voice of reason between the standoff. The tension was nearly unbearable and as thick as frozen butter.

"No" She said with tears coming to her eyes. "If you won't man up and get us some food then I'll just take it." She fired a shot and it struck Jared in the chest right above his AR-15 spare magazines. It knocked him backwards, but he was still able to pull the trigger firing several rounds into her, killing her instantly. She dropped to the ground with blood spewing out of her wounds. John screamed like a banshee as she fell. He ran towards Jared wanting to tackle him but Jared fired several more rounds into the charging newly widowed man. It was over in a second. The man fell forward and hit face first into the frozen dirt. Lanterns in several houses fired up including Gwen's. Daisy ran out the front door with her rifle not knowing what was going on.

"JARED!?" She yelled in to the night. "WHERE ARE YOU?" Her voice trembled with fear and adrenaline.

"I'M OVER HERE. STAY WHERE YOU ARE!" He was out of breath. With the armor stopping the bullet it still knocked the wind out of him and hurt like hell. He bent down to pick up the pistol. It was just a .380 caliber. No match for his Scorpion steel core armor. Dogs all around started barking like crazy at the rifle fire. With both weapons in hand he walked back home to a frightened Daisy standing at the door with rifle raised.

"It's me. Lower the gun and get inside". He wants to check his body and gear. People started to walk outside, several flashlights could be seen surveying and searching the area. He would need to meet with the neighbors in the morning first thing and explain his side of the story. Walking inside everyone was up and asked him what happened. "Damn people were trying to steal from us and I confronted them. That crazy bitch shot me", He pointed to the hole in his plate carrier. "So, I defended myself."

He slid his gear off to relax. He would have a nice bruise in a day or so. Time for some instant coffee, Irish style to calm the nerves. Sleep wasn't happening tonight. Just wait until the others see the bodies. He did not want to put up with their two cents.

29.

8 a.m. Arrived too soon. People in the neighborhood were moving about. Some saw the bodies and immediately freaked out calling for all the others to come out. That was his que. Time to face the gauntlet. He grabbed his plate carrier and put it on. Someone might want vengeance. Grabbing his rifle and walking outside with everyone but the kids following him. Someone saw him in military grade gear and raised their voice, so everyone would look at him.

"Allow me to explain this please." He waited for the whimpers, crying, and yelling to stop before continuing.

Several moments went by before someone finally asked him what he had to say.

"Last night I caught John trying to steal my chickens. My alarm scared him off and I know it was him because I watched him run straight inside his house. I went over immediately and confronted him about it. He denied it, but his wife came out demanding I give over my stuff to them because they were hungry. I said no. She then raised her weapon and shot me", pointing to the bullet hole, "I defended myself and shot back. John tried to attack me, and I defended myself yet again. It's that simply. It doesn't sound like it, but it is."

The crowd went silent and couldn't believe this had happened.

"Any questions?" Jared asked the crowd.

"Why did you confront him if he didn't get anything?" a little man with rim nosed glasses asked.

"To let him know I wouldn't tolerate it. And neither should any of you," pointing to the crowd.

"You should have gone to the police about this. You're not a cop." Another said.

Jared couldn't believe what these people were saying even after he told them she shot him. Apparently, he was the bad guy here.

"She shot me and I defended myself just like any of you would have. I don't see any way to get a hold of ANY law enforcement at 2 a.m. Do you?" He asked, and heads started nodding. Maybe they were coming around.

"You have chickens? Do you have any eggs?" a little old lady asked.

"Yes, I can spare some only if you are willing to trade. I will not just give them out. Eggs only, absolutely no chickens."

Angry murmurs started. Some didn't want to trade. They only wanted him to give them something for nothing. Because he had something and they didn't. Some were understanding and wanted to trade. That was a good start. The others could be trouble, so he would have to be extra careful now. Jared did agree to alert the authorities and get an ambulance out here to collect the bodies.

30.

Soon after the meeting Jared drove the accord to the hospital in an attempt to get an ambulance to collect the bodies and file a report. Being away from the city and in the county, there were several farms on the way towards the hospital. He wondered how they would do with all the people getting hungrier by the day. Cows were grazing in the open pasture with only a small, waist high barbed wire fence keeping them in. Great for cattle, not so much for humans. They could easily get through it and kill one of them. The farmer would need to keep a close count on them every day. Maybe these places will help turn the tide in a month or so when it's time to plant seeds. They could let volunteers trade labor now for food later when it was time to harvest. He would stop in one day and ask. Grass hasn't started to grow much yet, it was still short even without people mowing. He assumed a lot of yards will be over grown in the summer. Gas wouldn't be wasted for such nonsense like a manicured yard anymore. He passed the ball field where Todd used to play T-ball growing up. Many good and cheerful days had been spent at that place. Snacks and drinks everywhere, kids laughing and adults having simple conversations and just enjoying a peaceful day. Now those same people didn't even want to look at you unless you had something they could use. Lexington had its share of problems like any other city, but it did seem like a place that could stick together instead of cracking under hard times. They even use to hold "vintage car" nights, where everyone would bring their cars to show off. The same with "bike night" and motorcycles. And even "night on the town" nights where people could just meet and mingle with each other. That seemed like another lifetime ago. This type of hard times had never happened to modern civilization in America.

The hospital was close. Just needed to merge north onto the highway for two exits and he would be there. He only saw three cars on the road and they were loaded down and heading south to go only God knows where. Probably headed towards a family members house that would better suite them. Hell, maybe one of those cars was another prepper bugging out to their bug out location.

"I hope they find what they're looking for", Jared really meant it.

Pulling onto the deceleration lane and going around a curve he stopped where a stop light was. Even with it just hanging there dead and swinging in the breeze, he still stopped and looked both ways as a just in case. People were horrible drivers before, now without help from lights they would just zoom on through. Nothing in either direction so he hit the gas. The hospital was the very next road from the light. He was nervous about what he had to do. He knew the truth but would anyone believe him. Or would he be arrested on sight? But he did have to take responsibility for his actions. The hospital looked like a fortress now. Boarded up windows, razor wire stretched in every possible direction, and armed guards moving around. How long until the fuel runs out here? Then what will they do?

Will they still stay or move again? The soldiers looked well fed. They must have had a mountain of MREs in the armory. Made sense to him. Parking the car, he left his pistol in the car, he didn't bring his plate carrier. That could've sent the wrong vibe to them and maybe shot him thinking he was a threat. Locking the door behind him he made his way towards the entrance and was immediately stopped and searched before he could say anything. A stalky black man with Corporal rank gave orders to the others as they searched him. That was the one he needed to talk to.

"State your name and business here" the Corporal said.

"Jared Glover." His voice became weak and his stomach turned into butterflies. It was hard for him to speak the rest. His mouth just wouldn't cooperate with his brain.

"What's your business?"

"I would like to report...." he just couldn't do it, confess to killing his neighbors even if it was self-defense. The whole place looking like a prison didn't help either.

"Business now or leave" the Corporal was getting aggravated.

"Two dead bodies. I need someone to come get them. I shot them in self-defense." Jared's knees were getting weak and it was hard to stand up straight.

"Burn them or bury them." The Corporal said with a harsh tone.

"What?" Jared didn't understand.

"No fuel to spare on the dead. Either burn them or bury them. The bodies are stacking up and we can't keep going to get them. We just don't have the room in the morgue." The Corporals tone softened. "We are doing the same thing here or disease will spread and make matters worse. No autopsies are going on. We just don't have the resources."

"Worse? How could it get worse? It has only been a few weeks and we are falling apart." Jared was stunned. His knees were getting back to normal. He had always thought about scenarios where something like this would happen, but to actually be IN the situation was completely different. The reality of it was heavy.

"I know it sucks. You know it sucks. Everyone is in the same boat and it all sucks. These are the orders from the mayor's office. Burn them or bury them." The Corporal said matter of factly."You can leave now."

As he turned and started walking the Corporal yell out, "Just be sure to identify them and where they were put or what you did with them as best as you can...for record purposes later."

He had read about dealing with the bodies from the post-apocalyptic books he use to read, but that was after a nuclear war or EMP that made travel very difficult. They still had ambulances but were only using them to transport the living. It made sense...kind of. And he knew they were right. It would just take some time to adjust to that way of thinking.

The drive back was depressing. Now he would have to deal with everyone and their thoughts and opinions about all of it. And once again wondering if the audience would believe him once he said the bodies needed to be dealt with and help wasn't coming.

And he was right. Once he got home he went over to the bodies that someone had covered up with a thin sheet, they were frozen stiff from the cold ground and freezing weather. Digging would be very difficult so he decided to burn them instead. He went around to all the houses and let everyone know about it and when it would happen, so they could pay their respects if they wanted. Every single person was absolutely disgusted by the thought. After an hour of collecting materials, Jared had built an area with all the necessary wood and some fuel to get it started. He built what he thought he remembered from movies about the Romans building a wooden bed and setting the bodies on top. It was hastily built by an amateur and looked terrible. It was time to move the bodies. Putting on gloves so he wouldn't get blood on him he was able to load them in a wheel barrel and push them to the cremation area. He tried as best he could to position the bodies to look like they were sleeping. Finally, he just decided it was pointless and covered them with the sheet. He fired one shot into the air signaling to everyone it was time to start. Only a few showed up. One man that showed up had a shotgun resting in the crook of his arms and he wasn't happy.

"I'm not going to let you do this. It's inhumane and I won't stand for it", it was the man with the rimmed glasses from earlier.

"Mayors orders. It has to be done before they start decaying."

"Says you. No one else has heard that. I think you want to destroy evidence, so you can't be blamed for their murder." the man racked a round into the chamber but didn't point it at him yet.

"It was self-defense. I had no choice." Jared was nervous. He really didn't want another shoot out in his mother's neighborhood.

"Again...says you. No witnesses so you can claim whatever you want." The man was getting agitated.

"Then you go into town for help and see what you get. Nothing. Nada. Zip." Jared didn't like to be threatened. He had his pistol on him but no armor. It was inside. Big mistake. "We are on our own for a while."

A few more people started to show up because of the commotion. Jared lit a match and the man leveled his gun.

"Put it out" he demanded.

"Don't point that at me" Jared said "This has to be

done."

A shot rang out as the man shot into the air, an attempt to make his point more valid. He started to rack another round in the chamber but was too slow. Jared pulled his pistol and shot him twice in the chest. The man fell where he stood as on lookers screamed in terror. Some ran away. Others just stood in shock and didn't know what to do.

"Damn it!" Jared cursed loudly at what just happened. He walked over and picked up the gun in case someone else wanted to try to kill him today. "Someone go tell his family."

"He lived alone" a woman spoke softly.

This was too much for one man to handle. He grabbed the dead man with the assistance from adrenaline and was able to stack him on top of the pile with ease. Jared lit a match and started the fire. Daisy and Abby watched the whole ordeal from the safety of the house through a window. Gwen stayed with the kids so they wouldn't be able to sneak off and watch the corpse burn.

31.

"We're leaving tomorrow" Jared said. "Pack everything you want to take with you and aren't afraid to leave behind."

"Why?" Gwen asked "The funeral was two days ago. I'm sure they understand now."

"I doubt you'll be back anytime soon so make sure you get everything you want." Jared ignored her statement. He had already radioed the group to let them know he would be rehoming his family but didn't say where over the radio.

"I don't want to leave" Daisy had tears in her eyes. This was their home.

"It's not safe anymore. These people are not our friends. Do you think they will accept me and us after I had to kill three of them in less than a day? People they've known for years? I've found a place that we can go to and not have to worry about dangerous neighbors." Jared didn't stop packing the entire time he had tried to talk sense into them. It was time for them to Bug Out. This wasn't the first time he had mentioned leaving their home behind, years ago he told them it may have to happen if it got bad enough. At the time and up until today they just thought it was talk and never really thought about leaving. They didn't put anyone on watch. Everyone was too busy packing the vehicles to the maximum capacity. Throughout the years of just driving around, Jared always kept an eye out for places and resources he could use in a desperate time. The place he was talking about has a better water source and fewer people close by.

At the dead end of Petrea road stood a two-story house with a full basement and a pond that looked to be the size of half of a football field. The house had been on the market for years now, but no one wanted it. It was the scene of a murder/suicide that had taken place and made it undesirable and apparently unsellable. This was great news for Jared's family, and it was closer to where his kids were staying as well. The windows down stairs would need to be fortified so the upstairs can be the watch area with a greater view point. It was visible now but, in the spring and summer the tree leaves will hide it better from the road and what few houses were on the same road. It did however have an old dog lot that was a 10x10 foot area he could put the chickens in. He assumed the pond had some fish in it but probably more frogs and snakes than fish. That was fine with him. Animal meat was meat. He had had frog legs before and it wasn't that bad. Kind of taste like fish he said at the seafood restaurant. The inside had been newly renovated to try and help sell it, but it just didn't work. They would move in immediately.

It was a good decision but wouldn't last long. Things deteriorated faster and faster. The local government such as the mayor had given up after his security just stopped showing up. The city was officially a lawless and government-less zone. Good people were being prayed on by the stronger gangs that just outnumbered them.

32.

Three weeks into the power outage and things were getting worse in Raleigh. Riots were constantly going on. Day and night. Buildings burning, cars wrecked, stores looted to the bare walls. Police and military members were deserting fast. They were too concerned about their families than protecting some fat cats. The state capitol had only received a few tanker trucks of fuel and a few semi-trucks full of food. The aid from other countries just wasn't enough for the 330 million Americans, even with what could be shipped from the Midwest states that hadn't been affected as hard. And even if it could be shipped, it wasn't processed and couldn't make it everywhere or to everyone. Few countries were willing to help including Australia, Japan, The U.K. and a handful of other small countries. Other countries were watching with a smile and toasting to our destruction.

The fuel that had been delivered was destined only to keep the capitol running, a few government buildings and an overly used, overly crowded, and even more overly exerted staff in one hospital. People were starving and dying but there wasn't much anyone could do. Reports across the country said many trucks had been hi jacked and seized by the desperate population. Farms had been ransacked. Thousands of people dead from violence. The country had not come together like everyone expected. A few small towns had closed themselves off from migrating city dwellers looking for resources. "Keep walking. No room here" is what they all would say to anyone that came near.

The governor had decided to try an attempt to get aid to the biggest cities but would need more people to keep it safe from bandits during travel. It was like tribal warfare. Gangs of people teaming up to rob and kill those that had what they wanted and needed. An individual family didn't stand a chance if they were to encounter them. With no one to enforce the laws and courts to put them on trial, anyone and everyone that wanted to do whatever they wanted...did it and didn't care. It would be many years until anyone that wasn't caught in the act to get arrested and thrown in jail. This was a hoodlum's paradise. Who knew how long the aid would last. It couldn't go on forever. How many millions of people would be dead at the end of this? Desperate times called for desperate measures.

33.

"*Across the United States panic and death has taken a toll. It has been two months since the cyber-attacks and power plant bombings. In all, of the 200,000 miles of high voltage transmission lines, an estimated almost 100,000 miles had been damaged. Of the 5.5 million miles of local distribution, power lines, an estimated 3 million miles and countless transformers have been knocked out. Of the nearly 8,100 power plants, more than a quarter of them has been attacked and destroyed with explosive devices. And the saddest number are the American casualties...the number is only an estimate, but authorities believe the death toll to be around 10 million. That number is expected to rise substantially over the next several months. The world watches in horror as violence, disease, and starvation ravage the country. There is no time frame for complete restoration. It will take years, experts believe, to build, ship, and install all new hardware to restore power. Several countries have taken credit for the attack. The new coalition consist of China, Iran, North Korea, Syria, and Pakistan. Chinese and Korean hackers were able to take down the power grid. Under direct supervision of Chinese special forces, 20,000 soldiers from all nations were already spread throughout the country and waited for the attack command to physically attack the power plants to prolong any restitution and rebuilding for years to come. This well-regulated attack has been condemned by the rest of the world and pushing us further into a World War 3. Only a few of the attackers have been caught. The rest are believed to have fled the country in waiting boats disguised as cruise ships on all sides. Even though Martial Law was declared a month ago by the President, it wasn't being enforced due to lack of personal and resources. Only a few places were actually able to do it. It is unclear on how long this will last and what will follow."*

Jared couldn't listen to it any longer so he turned off the hand cranked emergency radio. He didn't know about the martial law part. Most places wouldn't be able to do that. Too many people and too few authority figures. It must've been why Lexington hadn't even tried it. This was one of those "*Don't tread on me*" areas. Probably more guns than people. He knew a lot of people in Lexington had died. Of the nearly 19,000 citizens, only 13,000 are believed to be alive. The entire world was going to shit. It was no secret that the United States had a wide range of enemies, but for them to hit us this hard and this efficient was unfounded...until a few months ago.

Make the country fight amongst themselves, kill each other off without putting a lot of your own troops at risk and then eventually just walk on in. Made sense. It made his blood boil. They were only able to stay at the new house for a few weeks before the crew decided it was in every one's best interest to consolidate into one area with their families. The house was great for a family or two, but not eight families.

Heading towards the small city of Tyro and away from the major highways that brought and influx of city people and their problems, they set up camp in a newly built gated community off Old Town Road. It was half way in between Lexington and Tyro. Tyro had a smaller population of just under 4,000 people. An eight-foot brick wall surrounded twelve houses. Only two had been moved into before it all happened. Several of the lots were still dirt and one house at the back end had not been completely finished yet. "Good" Jared thought. It wouldn't be on any maps yet.

Upon arriving at the new houses, they were confronted by someone shooting at them. The third house down and on the left, a man was shooting from his front door and missing every shot he took. What luck. They would need to secure that house immediately before he did get a lucky hit. John Ocwen had been a lifelong hunter, so he became the crew's "sniper". He maneuvered himself behind his vehicle and laid on the ground to make himself as small as possible and not let the shooter aware of his position. His radio crackled,

"Don't kill him. He may have some information about this area. He obviously doesn't know what he's doing," James ordered.

"Roger that" he responded.

With the crack of the .270 Winchester hunting rifle from less than 100 yards away. He was easily able to shoot the pistol from the man's hands. Dropping the gun, the man grabbed his hand in agony and the crew made their move. All but Dwayne the nurse, the crew's medic, fanned out and bounded from cover to cover like they've drilled many times in the past, they quickly made it to the house where a woman was hovering over the wounded man.

"Leave us alone," she cried as she tended to what Jared assumed was her husband.

"We'll talk in a minute." Jared barked back then told the crew "secure the house."

James moved in and the crew swept the house to secure it from any further hostiles. In the upstairs bedroom was a small child crying in a closet holding a stuffed teddy bear. The kid couldn't have been more than six years old. The woman began fighting as they moved through the house, but Pete and Martin kept her in the front room with the injured man. They brought the little boy down and he ran into his mother's arms scared and crying.

"What do you want now?" The wounded man

whose name was Walter asked unsure of his captors. "We gave you everything last time. We have nothing left."

"I don't know what you're talking about." James said. "We thought this place was abandoned so we were checking it out."

"You're not with those crazy thugs that keep coming back?" The woman named Jessica asked.

"Not us. We're coming from Lexington and needed to get away from that place." Jared said trying to ease her nerves.

"Lets get you fixed up. We have a nurse." James radioed for Dwayne Cruz to come inside to help.

Dwayne entered the house and began his work on the man's right hand. It was just cut and had a few pieces of metal from the damaged pistol but nothing major.

"Nice place. Yours?" Dwayne wanted to befriend them with some light and casual conversation.

"Yea it's ours. We were the first to move in when they were still working on this area. The only other family here left after the thugs came around and stole everything. We wanted to stay. This was our home." Walter said softly. He seemed to be a frail man with a thin body. Everyone was getting thinner, but this guy was getting bad.

"What did you do for a living before all of this

happened?"

"I was an accountant."

James and Jared assumed it had to be some sort of desk job.

"How many in the group that came?" James wanted to know.

"Too many. We just thought you were some we haven't seen before. That's how many." Walter was obviously frightened for his family.

Jared pulled James to the side. We need to setup a defense before anything else. I've seen two gates. The one we came in at and the rear gate. We'll need to completely block one and set up observation posts at the front. We're off the road a little so it shouldn't be too conspicuous. The road goes through the rear gate and looks to loop around both sides and merges back into the road at the front gate. Shouldn't be a problem though."

"And when those guys come back?" James asked.

"We'll be ready and kill every last one of them if we have to." Jared had already started thinking up a plan that he wanted to put into action. "I left the last place just for a new place the crew could setup somewhere and we could all have each other's backs. I didn't leave it to just keep running. This place here is going to be where I stay. It's a good location."

34.

A few days into the new housing area, the families had started to settle in. Each family had their own house. Todd, Gloria, and Linda had to move in and they had their own place. Her mom had died from a heart attack a few weeks ago and they didn't want to stay there. It was smart to bring them along. Now Jared wouldn't have to use extra fuel just to check on them and take them the already dwindling supplies. This just made sense and was more practical. Now he could concentrate on the everyday stuff instead of constantly thinking about their safety. Jared stayed with Gwen and the others.

The back gate had been reinforced with some abandoned cars that were nearby. They had to pull them in with the War Pig and push them into place, so no one could just ram the gate so easily. In every home on the second floor a look out post had been erected inside. This would keep the inexperienced fighters above ground level in case of an attack. The windows had been boarded up with the wood from the unfinished house. It was hard work but necessary to keep them safe. A creek was spotted about a hundred yards to the east of the compound. They made a dam for the creek to puddle into one area, so a pump would be more efficient. The overflow just allowed it to continue in its original path once it was high enough. The War Pig had a built-in air compressor for the air brakes, so they were able to connect to it and use a small pump they had come across to pump water into the compound. They need a way to get it into the homes easier. Maybe a gravity fed way. They'll figure that out after the area was secured better, this setup was just temporary.

Jared setup up a way to eliminate most of a hostile force if they managed to get into the compound, the deadly L-shaped ambush. Catching them in cross fire would throw them off guard and make them panic. Sharpshooters from the high grounds could pick them off as well. Using a few more cars and positioning them about twenty yards into the gate and using a few more to go down the right side, they could put up a nasty fight. A popular quote among gun fighters was,

"If you find yourself in a fair fight, your tactics suck."

This was noteworthy and always should be thought about when planning an attack or a defense. Things were going smoothly for a change. It was Mid-April and was time to start planting a garden. It would have to big enough to feed thirty-five people. Jared, Todd, Gloria, Linda, Daisy, Gwen, Abby and her three, James and his girlfriend and their one child, Dylan, his wife and their three kids , Dwayne his wife and their two kids, Martin his wife and one kid, John his wife and one kid, Pete his wife and one kid, Billy, and the new three members Walter his wife Jess and their one kid. It was a miracle that Walters family had survived this long. None of the crew and their families have died of starvation or sickness because of all their advanced planning. A little bit put back over time can build into an impressive stock. If only everyone would've thought like they did. Jared always told everyone he knew to have at least one month's provisions put aside. It would soften the blow if anything happened. Yet they didn't. One of Jared's coworkers that use to pick on him about his lifestyle had been killed trying to loot a grocery store at the last minute to feed his family. Jared had heard about it from one of the other workers he'd ran into at the community board. It was very sad news but something that was expected from the unprepared. That was life. As harsh as it had seemed.

They would plant several gardens a few weeks a part. This would allow them to dig a root cellar deep in the ground to keep things as fresh and long as they could. Dehydrating was another option by using the solar panels on the War Pig to power a dehydrator. Spreading the planting out a few weeks apart allows them to get more and waste less. They would use every bit of the yards they could. Gone were the days of useless, manicured, nonedible lawns. Walter and his family were adjusting just fine. Their little boy ran around with the other kids. They played but also had chores. Everyone did. Hoeing the ground for a garden was hard work and everyone had to chip in. The crew mainly did security but still had to pitch in for the manual labor.

A few weeks had gone by and the crops had tiny little plants coming up. A promising view everyone was excited about. Jared had kept them healthy and fed with plenty of wild greens. Dandelion salad with clovers and plantains were common and filled with vitamins. Canned and freeze-dried foods were holding out because they were rationed. Everyone had their own stock but did help each other out with trading and doing communal meals. It was getting to be like a big family. Billy and Martin were on watch duty at the front gate in the first houses attic window, the rear gate didn't need someone watching it because it was completely blocked. They were in pairs to keep from falling asleep and relieve each other for bathroom breaks. The watches were on six-hour rotations.

A car pulled in slowly down the road and close to the gate. They could see it had four people occupying it but couldn't tell if they were armed. The passenger got out and walked to the fence and tried opening it. It didn't budge.

"HELLO!?" the man shouted. He didn't know he'd already been spotted, and the crew was gearing up.

Jared was the first to the gate with no gear on except his pistol. He didn't want people thinking they had valuable stuff inside. The rest hung back out of sight but ready for action if needed. They were already at their predecided spots and waited.

"Hello, what can I do for you?" Jared asked.

"Why is the gate closed?" the man asked.

"This is my home. I'd like to keep it secured." Jared insisted on it.

"Never been locked before." the man had sleeve tattoos on both arms and wore a tattered muscle shirt with pants stained with grease. A pistol on his hip and what looked to be a machete on his back.

"You used to live here?" Jared wanted to question him with what little knowledge he had of the area.

"Nope, but I have some friends that were living here a few weeks ago and their taxes are due." The man was confident.

"Taxes? For what?" Jared wasn't feeling right. Something in his gut went off like a siren.

"Well don't you worry about it. There was a man, woman, and a kid here. Are they still?" The dirty man looked through the gate rails trying to see around. "I see you've been busy. Too much work for one man. That's intriguing." Black teeth showed through his twisted smile. "Guess I'll take your word about it. Have a good day."

Jared pulled the radio from his pocket and stepped to the side as the man walked back towards the car and said into the walkie, "Trouble. Don't let them leave."

The first shot went into the driver's side of the wind shield catching the driver in the throat. The dirty man turned around in shock as bullets poured into the car killing the three other occupants. He went for his gun but was too slow, Jared shot him in the stomach and he doubled over.

"Cease fire, secure the area" James barked into the radios they all carried.

Jared opened the gate as the man tried to compose himself and sit up against the car. Blood came from his mouth as he sat in disbelief. Jared ran over and kicked the gun away then pulled the machete from his back. Looking into the car it was obvious that no one had a chance. John, Pete, and Dylan made it to the gate and setup a small perimeter in case any others were coming.

"Get Dwayne and his kit to the surgical room", which was just a back bedroom that the medical supplies were stored, Jared ordered. Chatter filled the radio waves as the other members started to coordinate with each other. They would deal with the bodies later. They drug the injured man into the surgical room and Dwayne went to work, at least enough to stabilize him so they could ask him some questions. Walter came in and was able to identify the man as one of the gangs Lieutenants.

"Why didn't you tell us they were collecting "taxes" from you. What did they want? And why didn't you tell us they'd be back soon?" Jared wanted answers now.

"They said they'd leave her alone as long as I got them things they could use", Walter teared up, scared of the repercussions that will follow. "I thought maybe if they saw all of you here, they'd just leave us alone for good."

"Get him out of here. I need to think." James was

furious. Those were details he needed to know. Jared escorted Walter back home.

An hour later, Dwayne had the man stable enough to talk. Using ammonia break open packets to keep him awake. James started,

"Who are you and what do you want?"

He didn't say anything.

"Ok, let's try something else," James took his pocket knife out and jammed it an inch into the bullet hole. It sent the man into a blinding, agonizing scream as he tried to escape. The duct tape they used to secure him to the bed was doing its job and holding.

"Where's your camp?" James asked with the blade still in the wound, "Or do I need to start twisting?"

The man opened the flood gates and started talking.

"We're at the country club a few miles east. We go around taking what we want." The man blubbered.

"And who is we?" James asked nicely but the blade was still buried.

"Convicts from the medium security prison in Lexington. Power went out and so did the electronic locks, we bailed. Come on, man. Don't do this." The pain was immense.

"You're dirty and raggedy looking, but you don't

act like a harden criminal." James said mockingly.

"I was just there for skipping out on child support, man. Pull the knife out." He cringed at any slightest movement James did.

"Hold on. In a minute. How many are there?", This was the main thing he wanted to know.

"Like fifty I think, I don't know the exact number." He relaxed when the knife was pulled out, it was a big relief even though the wounds still hurt. "This mean you gonna let me go?"

"One thing I've learn from movies. Never leave loose ends." With that said, he flicked his wrist severing the arteries in his neck. It only took a minute for the dirty convict to gurgle then bleed out. It was all over.

"I wished you had told me you were going to do that before I wasted my medical dressings on him," Dwayne said annoyed. "And who's going to clean this up?"

"Sorry", That was all James said as he left the room.

35.

They wanted to see how Lexington was fairing. It had been nearly three months since the blackout and two days since the convicts had come through. No sign of trouble from the others yet. But they would need to be dealt with and soon. They wanted to see if the National

Guard or police in town would be able help. They would need to report it and try to get some backup.

Jared, Daisy, Billy, and John loaded into the quad cab F-250. All were fully geared up, even Daisy who had a mix of gear that was donated by everyone in the crew. They were ready to go into town. They looked like a group of misfits from an apocalypse movie. They pulled out of the gate and headed west towards Lexington. It was a warm sunny day and they were glad for it. Not sure how glad they would be in the humid and hot summer in a few months, but for now it was perfect weather for a car trip. Even if it was only a few miles. This would be an interesting adventure nevertheless. It took them about fifteen minutes to make it to the outskirts of town. Pulling up to the towns welcome sign, it had been spray painted over. No one had any respect anymore. They passed into the town limits and eased down the road at a steady 35 mph. Slow so they could look at as much as they could without having to stop. The place was a wreck, passing the State Highway patrol's office and DMV they had been burnt to the ground. Really couldn't blame them for the DMV part. Jared would've love to have done that himself and their three-hour waiting time. They either couldn't hold them off or abandoned their post long ago. They kept driving and saw the familiar sights, the biscuit king he often went to, the farm and garden, and one of his favorite places in the old Coke-a-cola factory, Christo's pizza and wings. It made him sad to see the windows busted out and trash everywhere. He really wanted some pizza, but he'd probably never have it again. They were getting closer to the center of town. Cars were pushed to the side of the road, trash littered every water drain. People just threw their garbage on the ground. No trash man would be by to collect it, so it didn't matter to them. Past the family video rental where he and his kids rented many movies and games together, the boost mobile store had been looted, he sarcastically wondered if the "No guns allowed" sign helped keep anyone from robbing them. Oh, the Irony he thought. Easing through the blind spots where stop lights used to be then speeding up. A few people were out and about riding a bicycle or pushing a shopping cart. They looked filthy and probably smelled even worse. The armory would be coming up soon, the road beside a church, he would take a left and go down a few hundred yards. Pulling into the parking lot it seemed deserted. The front door was wide open, and a few torched Humvees could be seen at the side of the building. "Looks like this place is empty. Anyone want to go inside and look around?" Just as he thought it was a big collective no. Time to move on. The situation seemed haunting and dire. If the guard gave up, then what else could they do? If big brother wasn't helping them, then did they really care about expendable civilians? I didn't look good.

"Keep your eyes sharp everyone", Jared said. This was eerily like the convoys he did in Iraq all those years ago. Weapons facing outwards with the windows down in case you needed to quickly engage a hostile enemy. The save-a-lot grocery store had been picked over and over even after it all had been moved. The library was coming up, they may want to go there one day for some informational books. Center of town was just another half mile up the road. There weren't any homes on this street, it was all businesses that had seen better days. Jared slowed the truck down as a road block came into view. It was placed at the four-way intersection at Lanier's hardware store. Several men were armed and standing guard. Jared slowed down so they wouldn't think he was a threat.

"HALT! WHO GOES THERE!?" the middle guard yells. Jared put the truck in park and got out slowly.

"I'm going to ask some questions. Daisy, you get in the driver's seat and if anything bad happens, just drive away fast." She nodded and moved over. He started walking towards them.

"Stop where you are," the guard didn't have to yell anymore. He wasn't dressed in military fatigues. Just civilian clothes and a shotgun. Both his flanks were the same thing. Civilian clothes but AR style rifles instead. "Who are you and what do you want?"

"Just information if possible" Jared exclaimed. "I was wanting to talk to someone at the police station. The National Guard station was abandoned."

"Yea, we know. Why do you need to see the police?"

"We came across some convicts that escaped the prison. They're held up in Tyro, killing people and robbing them. We need help." Jared wanted help desperately. This couldn't go on.

"With the looks of your vest, I'd say you're doing fine." The guard said sarcastically. The other guards got a good chuckle from it.

"Can you help or not?", Jared was getting impatient. "Is there any way we can talk more face to face?"

"You're fine were you are for now."

"Why is main street blocked off?" Jared asked.

"New Mayors orders. We were getting raided and it had to stop here and now." He pointed east to west. "Three blocks both ways and from here to West MLK Jr Boulevard. Blocked off and under heavy guard. All side streets and alleys have been sealed. Total containment."

"New mayor? Where's the old one?" Jared looked in the directions he had pointed.

"He quit. Said screw it. Packed up a bunch of the towns supplies and took off. He's to be shot on sight just an FYI."

"How are Y'all getting by?" Jared asked.

The guard was getting noticeably antsy "I won't reveal that to any stranger."

"Stranger? I've lived here twenty years." Jared

was upset at that comment.

"Got any ID on you?"

He did have his license and conceal carry permit that was always kept in a pocket beforehand just in case he was pulled over while heading to a range. He shows them to the guard who seemed convinced.

"Good. By this concealed permit I know you've been vetted, and finger printed with an FBI background check." He gave them back and looked behind him. "Open the gate."

The middle car moved to allow the truck inside. Jared motioned for the truck to ease inside the gate slowly. Once inside the car moved back into position.

"I'll escort you to the new mayor's office, so you can speak with him about the convicts. We've been hit by them as well. Not so much since the walls have been put up." The guard jumped in the back of the truck and pointed the way.

"How did you get people together and do all of this?" Jared asked. He sat in the back with him.

"Handed out what the mayor couldn't carry as payment for work. He had all kinds of stuff squirreled away in the basement of the office. Leaving us to starve. Saying it was for the good of the community that he stayed fed and alive. Food is rare and a great motivator." He explained a few things Jared had questions about but avoided others. The ride was short. The businesses looked to be turned into living arraignments for those who wanted to live there. Exchange labor for food and security. People were out more here. Cleaner looking as well. The new mayor's office was the old court house from the 1800's that had been turned into a historical monument. On top of the court house, Jared could see the barrel of a machine gun on a stack of sandbags. He felt a little safer here. He wondered what all could be done in just the city limits.

36.

A man in military pants and boots but with a civilian shirt sat at a desk looking over a large paper. It looked to be an outline of the cordoned off city area. Jared was escorted in as the others waited outside with the truck.

"Mr. Mayor. This gentleman knows where the escaped convicts are. They are having trouble with them in Tyro." The guard stands to the side as the mayor stands up to greet Jared.

"Thank you for coming forward. Those bastards have caused this town a lot of unnecessary grief. My name is Joe Hansel, former 1SG of the local National Guard unit stationed here."

"Former? We drove by the armory and it was a wreck," Jared relaxed a little "Figured everyone deserted and ran home."

"Close. Nearly half left. 150 were stationed here. We were the largest in the area. 132 showed up when called. Now all I have is 65 dedicated soldiers including me. I should say former soldiers now. The federal government called us to Raleigh but only twenty went. The others deserted. Can't say I blame them. The money stopped. Even if it didn't, it was just worthless paper now. The rest of us wanted to stay and help these people. We couldn't just let the die here. That would break the oath we took. Which is also why I won't enforce that silly Martial Law stunt."

It was an emotional conversation. Being a former military man himself, Jared understood what he was talking about.

"It was too obvious of a target and too small to live in for the long hall for all of the troops. We emptied out and set up shop here. When the people in town saw us moving, they were immediately concerned. We reassured them we'd stay around and help out. It just snowballed into this once *real* leadership took over. The mayor was a coward. He made a few speeches then held up in his building to stay away from the people he vowed to serve. Disgusting." He took a deep breath and sighed out loud,

"How many people are here in the safe zone?" Jared wasn't sure he wanted to know.

"Actually inside? I'd say 2,000. There's more outside but we don't have an accurate count. The cemetery is basically a mountain of bodies. We stopped

115

counting around 3,000. That's just the ones brought in. No one knows the actual number. We estimate around 8,000. Starvation in the middle of flu season in the middle of winter. We never stood a chance." Joe walked over to the window. "They hit us in the most brutal way. At least we could've seen a nuke launched and had a chance to shoot it down. But this...this was never seen coming. The cyber-attack, yea we had professionals keeping them at bay every day. But the physical attacks? Never saw it coming. They just walked in and did whatever they wanted to do then left."

This was a depressing conversation. Jared didn't like it, but it had to happen.

"Americans killing Americans over beans or a can of corn. Embarrassing. We are better than that. We need to stick together and keep each other safe. And we need all the help we can get." The new mayor wanted allies.

"We won't move into the safe zone. But we can still help each other out. My crew can be an observation post and report anything we see to you. Just give us a frequency for the ham radio and we'll be good to communicate. Just help us take out the convicts so we can sleep better at night."

"Deal" they shook hands.

37.

Jared walked outside and gave them the good

news. They loaded up and left. A lot of planning would be needed so they would need to recon the area. Mayor Joe would send a small group to do that and get back with Jared's crew. He doubted they would be involved in the actual assault, but he was glad for the intel Jared was able to give him. Jared could live with that decision. Let the younger fellows take care of this. He just hoped the casualties were zero, that was wishful thinking and wouldn't happen.

38.

One week after the talk with the new mayor, the assault was a success. The convicts barely put up a fight against actual warriors. They were only use to picking on those that couldn't defend themselves. An actual experienced, well-armed force just ran them over. A few causalities on the mayors' side. Two dead and six wounded. Most of the convicts were killed and twelve were taken prisoner. They would be on the newest work force addition in Lexington...the chain gang. It would be wrong to outright murder them once they'd given up, so why not use them as a resource to improve what they tried to destroy? Jared only heard a few details. All he was concerned about was the threat level was down and the bullies were gone. This would make their lives easier for the moment.

Mayor Joe had a good standing with some 2,000 safe zone residents. He had organized the walls, labor, and guards that kept them safe. He proved his loyalty by not leaving when ordered. His now 63 men were stretching thin. It was time to get the civilians that were 18 and older to become a force to be reckoned with. Training would be needed just in case an assault on the zone happened. It could come from any number of threats. Towns nearby organizing to feed their own or a religious cult where a mad man could convince desperate people to do his own bidding. It has happened all throughout history. People will do anything to ensure they live to the next day. Primal instinct.

Nearly 600 men and women volunteered for the town's forces. From ages 18 to 60. Some of the older folks said they may be near retirement age, but they were still full of piss and vinegar. Especially since there was no more social security to help them out when they would be able to claim it. This was their new retirement plan. The new mayor had done what everyone thought was impossible. He brought Lexington back together. He gave them the confidence to work towards rebuilding the city they called home. Being it was the south, many of them knew how to use a gun. The others would learn in time. They would need to practice and drill for emergencies and defense positions. Keeping evil beyond their borders. They were able to claim enough of the spoils of battle from the convicts to keep going for a few more weeks. Calorie intake was down drastically for those who couldn't provide a service of any type, and the fighters and workers had only half of what the normal calorie intake should be. Everyone was dropping weight, but they were alive. Food was scarce and getting even more scarce with every day that pasted. Every inch of open yard or flower bed and even the roofs of the buildings were turned into garden spaces. It was just the beginning of the growing season and the seeds have been planted. Now it was just a matter of time and keeping these good people fed until harvest time. What the former mayor had squirreled away would only last another week if that. He would send out scavenger parties to see what could be found. It would have to do for now. He couldn't stand the thought of Americans starving but it was inevitable. Even the hunters and gathers were coming back with less and less. Using books from the library they were able to start identifying wild edibles, but nature only provided so much.

39.

Month four and there was no end in sight. No convoys to rescue Lexington and the survivors within from the hell outside. No fuel had been delivered as promised. No food. No medicine. Where was FEMA and all their funding and supplies? They were a joke. They couldn't handle one city when a hurricane hit. Jared had been right for prepping the way he did. Using his time and money to learn new skills. He'd just wished more people would've as well. The gated community they've been living in for weeks now was now dubbed "The Compound". Simple and easy name. Their gardens had shot up like weeds. Thick and full. Not many failures but a few plants did die.

Todd and all the other children had responsibilities such as going through the gardens every day and weeding. Making sure the chickens were fed and watered, collecting eggs and several other chores. Everyone had to do their part to keep the compound clean and running.

They were able to get a hold of several more solar panels from an undamaged solar farm that wasn't too far away. Pete's skills as an electrician made it all possible. Jared knew enough to get the ones on his truck set up, but anything larger was out of his skills set. They couldn't keep cranking up the truck to use the built-in air compressor, it used too much fuel. Jared had already gone back for the hidden kerosene. It was in the tank being used for fuel now. The diesel was long gone. Soon they would start draining motor oil from abandoned cars or start trying to figure a way to make biodiesel. That would be the better option. Cleaner and easier in the motor. The other vehicles they came in were running on fumes. Gas was nowhere to be found. All the cars they've come across had been drained already. It was time to find more old diesels to fix up and try to drive around.

Gloria had been tasked with helping out with the guard shifts. She was old enough and has proven herself to be a good shot. Under her dads wishes she would only watch from the high grounds and not in any other way. Times were different, and kids would be growing up faster than they were used to, but she was still his little girl and wouldn't take no for an answer. She didn't have any type of body armor or gear to wear. That was on the "to buy" list but budget always got in the way. During the final weeks that he thought everything would go down, he'd put all his funds into getting the War Pig ready for Bugging out.

Keeping the kids occupied and tiring them out with chores helped keep the "I'm bored" complaining to a minimum. Although, they still were able to play the same repetitive games on their tablets when they were charged. Watching a DVD on the portable players were good for raining days. The movie rental place wasn't hit too bad and they made a trip to grab some movies to keep from over watching the ones they already had. It was a nice distraction from time to time to sit and watch something even if it was on a small screen.

Keeping good hygiene was a must. The toilet paper was about a quarter of the way gone. The bar soaps were doing good as well. They had nearly 180 bars of it left. The pump had been pumping into several 55-gallon drum barrels. Each house had one set on the roof with pipes coming out and into the bathroom for a quick shower. They used garden hoses strung out, one for each house. It was quicker to just switch the hoses at the pump then run from barrel to barrel with one hose. The houses were on septic tanks, so they were able to use the toilets when filled and never flushed just for pee, only turds following the saying *"If it's yellow let it mellow, if it's brown flush it down"*. They would need to find another pump or two to try and make it faster to fill the barrels by filling more than one at a time.

The local hardware store had been looted of course, the cash register was hit first probably, but not much had been taken other than the high dollar coolers they had and a few other items. The crew didn't care about that stuff, just the building materials they could use to make life a little more bearable. The creek had a steady flow, but they didn't trust the clean looking water. They did use filters for the water when drinking and cooking. A distillery would be a better option and they could do a lot of water at a time. The filter would be going bad eventually, so it was time to start thinking about that.

There were days when there really wasn't much to do. The area in the middle had formed into the central hangout spot when the weather was nice. A fire pit, a few chairs, and a swing had been pulled there to make it seem more normal, like a relaxing pre-blackout Saturday night just hanging out. Friends and family just trying to make it through another day. They would talk about the good times they used to have and the good food they used to eat. Everyone had that one favorite food they all missed. At least they weren't starving like most of the country was. It all had an upside if you looked hard enough.

Gwen and few of the other women had went back to more of the traditional roles like cooking and laundry. It was what they felt comfortable doing. They could help on watch if they wanted. Both Daisy and Gloria did. The others didn't care for it. Doing laundry the hard way of scrubbing by hand made it to where people wore their clothes for several days at a time to cut back on the detergent and the labor.

Life was going well for the moment.

40.

Another beautiful day had started. The daily routines continued uninterrupted. Watchful eyes acting like guardian angels sat in the windows. A few vehicles could be heard passing. They were off the road about a hundred yards, far enough they always hoped no one would decide to turn down the road with a "no outlet" sign. They had considered using a toy drone with a built-in camera for quick recon of the roads but decided against it, it would draw too much unwanted attention from passersby. Dylan's oldest son was eight and a drone enthusiast. He would always do small work around their houses for money to improve it. No need to risk it. The chores had gotten done that morning, so they wouldn't be in the sun all day moving around and could have a little fun. The children ran around, Todd watched them as best he could and kept them safe. He was happy to do it for the most part. Wanting to do watch with the grown-ups, this was the next thing to it, so it would do for now.

They could hear a car speeding down the road but couldn't see it directly until it had turned down their road. Speeding up until it came into view, the driver must have seen the car blockade too late and tried to brake but instead rammed into the two staggered cars that protected the gate from being rammed directly. Metal crunched and twisted as the impact stopped the speeding car. The three cars were now entangled all in one pile. It looked as if the newest car was just a crumbled-up piece of tin now. The ear-splitting crash had everyone in the compound stopped in their tracks. People came out of the houses to see what was going on.

"Watch dogs, what's going on?" James asked into the radio.

"A car just tried to ram us. Gear up, prepare for possible attack." Jared had been on watch with Gloria, teaching her what he could remember from his standing post days in Iraq and what to look for.

Children were rushed inside as every adult grabbed a weapon and prepared for the worst. Most hunkered down in their homes. The crew plus Walter and Daisy went to their assigned positions and awaited further instructions. James, with weapon raised at the ready, made his way towards the crash.

"Any movement?" James asked.

"None I can see" Jared replied. "Stay sharp."

James slid the gate open just enough for a person to fit and moved towards the car. Fuel was leaking but no signs of a fire yet. No movement in the car. He walked up to driver's door weapon still up, the driver was just a kid. Looked to be no more than thirteen years old. He must've been running from something or someone, or possibly just joy riding.

"It's just a kid. Must've been too much car for the

poor soul." James voice was anguished. The bloody body was pinned into the car. It would take the fire departments Jaws of Life to cut him out. Death must've been instant. James was actually glad for that part. No pain and suffering.

"Get back inside. We'll push the wreckage off to the side somewhere out of sight." Jared told everyone to stand down. It was tragic but not threatening.

Jared was relieved from his Watch dog stand early so he could use the War Pig to move the cars. All he had to do was hook to the front car that the kid was in. The cars were so mangled together he just had to pull one and the rest followed. He didn't even bother looking at the victim. Nothing he wanted to see. Broken glass and bits of metal needed to be swept up to prevent tire damage if they had to leave. Blood had seeped out and onto the road. It mixed with gas as the cars were moved. Pulling the cars as far off the road as possible, Jared wanted to bury the kid, but it wasn't possible. That was enough excitement for one day.

A few hours later, another car was heard driving close by. This one slowly pulled in and stopped a ways away from the gate. A woman emerged and walked towards the compound and made it to the gate. John and Daisy were on watch and reported it immediately to James and Jared. They both walked towards her, they were just wearing normal clothes. Nothing tactical at the moment. Dressing like that all the time was getting old. Sometimes, you just needed something comfortable like shorts and a pair of crocs, but always with their pistol belts on.

"Hello, sorry to bother you," The woman was very nice and soft toned.

"What can we do for you?" James asked her.

"My son has run off. I saw the fresh tire marks in the grass up here. He took one of my cars and just left. Have you seen him?" The woman seemed calm. Too calm for someone with a missing kid. Especially in these times.

James and Jared traded looks. They knew it must've been the same kid from the crash.

"Ma'am, we've got some bad news," Jared said, "You'll have to follow us."

James spoke into the radio saying they were going to escort this lady to the crash. Watch dog post confirmed it.

They opened the gate and went out closing it behind them. Just a few yards to the right and into the tree line, a small dirt path had been made by the cars being pushed earlier. It was only about twenty feet in the wooded area. Jared and James stayed back at the road as they told her what happened. They pointed to the cars and said he was still in there. She walked over to the car and looked inside. She showed no emotion like a true mother would.

Jared whispered to James "Something is off here, man. It doesn't feel right."

"I know" James agreed, "She's not crying or screaming. Not even in shock. Like it's not even a big loss to her."

"She looks pretty healthy if you know what I mean." Jared pointed out.

"Did you see the kid?" James asked quietly.

"Nope. No urge to see that."

"The kid was skin and bones. Puny, almost like from a concentration camp from World War 2. It was no wonder he died on impact. No cushion." James was getting suspicious.

They stopped talking as the woman turned to them and walked back.

"Yea that's him alright. Damn shame. Boy never did have a lick of sense." Her tone went harsher like she was disappointed in something. Not the caring voice a mother would have. Or even a distant relative.

"Would you like for us to try and get him out, so you can bury him?" Jared offered.

"Nah. It's fine," She thanked them then got into her car. As she put it in reverse, James got onto the radio.

"Dylan, get your kids drone in the sky now!" His voice was urgent. The drone had been out since they were messing with the idea of using it, so it could be in the air fast. It had a camera on it that relayed to the owner's smart phone via an App. Dylan kept his phone charged so his wife could look at the family photos they took and to keep occupied with some games that were downloaded.

"Ok, it's ready. What do you need it for?" Dylan asked.

They were back in the compound and made it to him. "Follow that car" Jared said. He looked around "I've always wanted to say that."

"That woman's up to no good" James replied. "Let's see where she goes."

"Hope it's close. This battery is small and won't last but twenty minutes or so." Dylan informed them. The drone rose from the ground and launched directly into the closest house and fell to the ground undamaged.

"What'd you do?" Jared asked in a panicked voice, "We're going to lose her. Get it back up." Dylan tried again but couldn't work it right.

"Quick, go get your boy to pilot this thing," James ordered and Dylan took off running. He was back in no time with kid in tow nearly pulling him to fast for the boy to stay upright.

He handed the controller to him and told him to get it in the air. The boy was ecstatic he got to play with the drone again. They quickly found the target and told him to follow high in the sky. They would stay with her as long as they could. She turned left on old town road and headed towards Tyro. Going to the end of Tyro road, she turned left again onto South Highway 150. She continued for another mile then turned left down a road no one was sure of the name, pulling into the fourth house on the right. Just in time, the battery was low, and it had to return or crash.

"Quick, take a screen shot of the area." James ordered. With the screen shot taken the drone returned home. "Fine job, boy. You did good."

The young boy smiled at the approval.

"That's a mighty fine toy you have there kid," Billy said as it landed.

"Toy? It ain't no toy." The boy's name was Jacob, spoke up obviously offended for an eight-year-old. "This is a Mavic Pro drone."

"Ok? So, it has a fancy name. Big deal." Billy instigated him on purpose.

"It's more than a fancy name. This bad boy has a 4.3-mile range and can go nearly 16,000 feet in the air for 27 minutes. I saved and begged for two years to buy this high-tech aerodynamic gizmo." He said flustered.

Dylan cut in, "How is it you know all of that down to the fine detail, yet you barely passed English?"

Jacob just smiled and skipped away sticky his tongue out at Billy. Basically, that was the kids equivalent to the middle finger.

There was a short meeting with every adult not on watch, they would fill them in later, about what they should.

"Let's look at what we know" James started. "She's overweight in a time where food is minimal, and sickness is at the maximum. That kid was nearly a skeleton and she showed no sad feelings at all towards someone she claimed was family. Something is definitely up, and I don't like it."

Gwen cut in "So are you saying what I think you're saying?"

"What?", Dylan's wife asked confused.

"A cannibal", Gwen said in a low voice.

"A cannibal?" Martin asked like he didn't believe it. "Here? In North Carolina? This isn't some backwoods country. We don't eat each other. That's a pretty extreme accusation."

"True but look at it this way. She's only a few miles away. A quick recon will settle our nerves. Hopefully, it's nothing then we leave her be." Jared wanted to be the level-headed neutral man. He didn't want to think something that grotesque would be anywhere near them.

"People are desperate. Weird shit goes down when people are desperate." Pete said from behind the crowd leaning against a wall. "I say let's go look."

"Any objections?" James asked looking at everyone. "No? Ok, we'll send out a small team to check her out."

"If we find out she's been eating the forbidden meat?" Martin asked hoping the answer was what he wanted.

"If you find indisputable proof then the team should engage" James said matter of factly. "Jared, Billy, and John will go as soon as they're ready. Make a plan then head out."

41.

The plan was simple. Take the phone to help recognize the area and park a few hundred yards away, move in on foot. Remain hidden and observe. Keeping in contact with the compound the whole time in case something was to happen, and they needed backup.

They all put on their full gear. It was go time. Loading into one of the smaller trucks they headed off. Following the same route she took, they stopped a few hundred yards away and hid the truck as best as possible from anyone passing by. Moving while staying in the tree line they made it to the road she had pulled down. From the tree line the neighborhood looked like one of those Homeowners association places. Where uptight and higher up the tax bracket people lived. They counted eighteen houses. All were three stories high and very nice. Attached garages, small yards over grown with weeds and grass. They looked to be abandoned. At least what they could see. They would need to observe longer to get a better feel for the situation. Finding a house that they were absolutely sure was abandoned, they moved in to set up an observation post to watch her house at all times. At least one of them would continuously have eyes on so nothing could slip through. They set up in one of the top bedrooms, making sure all the windows elsewhere were blocked completely. A few hours had passed. The car was still in the driveway, no movement outside. Night was coming in fast. They would work out some sort of sleep order, always keeping at least one up. Jared would take first watch for four hours, then Billy, then John. Once the other two were settled in, Jared would start the clock. Within the first hour of his watch, about 9 pm, he saw the movement of light as the front door opened. The woman walked out with a garbage bag and a shovel. Jared was close enough to shake Billy's leg to wake him up.

"Movement, wake up John as well." Jared said in a whisper.

They all three were at the window in the pitch-black room behind dark curtains pulled slightly to the side. Just enough to see what she was doing. The plump woman began digging a hole, once she was satisfied with the depth she dropped the bag into it and covered it back up. Patting the top, she turned and walked into the house and shut the door.

"What do you think?" John said lowly.

"We need to know what that was." Jared began to move and get his radio out. He needed to report this in and let them know they would be checking it out. "Billy, you're up. Stay low and go find out what that was. Bring it back but fill in the hole so she doesn't know someone was here."

"Got it." Billy was still in his gear. They wouldn't take it off, so they could move at a moment's notice. As silently as he could, he slipped down stairs and out of the back door. Moving from cover to cover, he moved closer to the intended area. Jared and John waited in the room, rifles in their laps, and ready to provide cover fire. Getting to the road, Billy got down in the prone position in the ditch and waited. He waited a few minutes, listening to his surroundings. He got up and crossed the road then back in the prone. *I'm up, he sees me, I'm down.* It was a military quick rush drill they had done many times. He'd never thought he'd actually use it. Low crawling on his stomach and inching his way closer, he made it to the hole. Digging with his hands took longer than if he'd had a shovel, and if he was standing up. But he did it. Pulling the bag from the dirt, he replaced what he could then left in the same manner as when he'd came over. Finally making it back in the house and up into the room. He needed to catch his breath. Doing all of this he had sweated up a storm. But the mission was a success. The bag sat on the floor, all three just stared at it. Did they really want to see what it was? Could they live with themselves if they just left?

Jared ripped opened the bag, human sized bones fell out. A small rib cage and a skull fell to the floor. They were stripped of all meat and were perfectly white. Cleaned to the point that it could've been a fake skeleton from a doctor's office. But why would she bury one if it was fake? It meant that it was real. John began to gag as he realized the truth, Billy dry heaved yet no vomit came. Jared just sat there. He'd seen bodies before overseas. But this was different. All he felt was rage. That someone could get this desperate. He stood up.

"Man up, boys. Time to move" Jared was at the door and ready to go. The others followed him. "Billy get to the back door so she can't leave. We'll go in the front." He didn't bother calling it in and letting them know. He wanted this to end now.

They moved across the road, spreading out and went to their places as quietly as possible. They wanted the element of surprise. Billy was at the back door, Jared and John was at the front. Jared stepped back to get enough power behind his kick. With a violent smash, the front door opened with a loud crash. A scream of panic came from the house, now it was time to find her. Jared went left and into the closest room, it was the living room. Flashlights on their rifles filled the rooms. It would nearly blind anyone who wasn't ready for it when it hit them directly. No need for night vision. This would need to go fast. Shock and awe, and she was definitely shocked. John peeled off to the right. It was the dining room. A door on the other side led into a room with a light already on. He moved closer to it, the woman came around the corner and buried a knife deep into his left shoulder. He screamed in shock and pain as she threw her weight into him knocking them both on the floor. Both hands on the knife she pushed it even deeper. All the way to the handle. Fumbling around he was able to roll her over onto her back, laying on top of her he pulled his pistol out, stuck it in her mouth pulling the trigger. She stopped fighting immediately. Her hands dropped instantly. Brains, blood, and skull fragments oozed onto the floor.

"I'm hit" He yelled as he holstered the gun and rolled off her. The knife was still inside. Blinding pain filled every nerve he had. Jared ran into the room to see his fellow crew member blooded and stabbed. The woman's body laid on the floor. Billy kicked opened the back door and made his way in after he heard John yell he was hit. John was able to remove his IFAK and start his own first aid. Jared leaned beside of him, "Stay here. We need to secure the rest of the house. Billy, on my six." With that they were gone. John sat up and shimmied over to the closest wall to help support him, so he could sit up better. He would need to leave the knife in, Dwayne would be able to remove it better and safer. Packing white, sterile dressings around it, flinching with every movement. It hurt...a lot. Not much blood was seeping out. The knife was acting like a plug, but he would still need to stabilize it, so it couldn't move around as much and do more damage.

Jared and Billy stayed together. The last thing they needed was another member going down. They swept the house, both down stairs and upstairs. No one else was here. The moved back down stairs and into the kitchen to look around. A plate was on the counter with a steak, or what looked to be a steak. A hand cranked meat grinder, the same that deer processors used, was mounted as well. In the top of the grinder little fingers were poking out. She was grinding all the small stuff up, so she wouldn't waste any and trashed the rest. A bowl labeled "bone broth" sat there with a spoon in it. It looked as if she boiled everything else. That explained why they were so clean when she buried them. A cold shiver ran down his spine. What kind of monster would do this? That's when he heard it. A low noise. Like someone who was too weak was calling out to him. It was coming from the door that went into the garage. They hadn't been in there yet. He grabbed the door handle and eased it opened, rifle up and flashlight on. What he saw would give him nightmares for years to come.

Animal cages lined the walls on all sides. The smell of death, shit, and vomit was enough to make him nearly put on his gas mask. In several of the cages, children of various sizes and ages were crammed in.

"BILLY!!" he screamed. He would need help.

Both physical and emotional. Billy ran through the door and just stopped cold. His mind couldn't believe what his eyes were showing him. Some looked to be half way healthy. Others were just living skeletons. Too weak to move. They just laid there.

"What the hell is this?" Billy waved his rifle around to use the light to see more. In a corner were piles of clothes and toys. A plastic storage tub had hair filling it. All of the kids were bald. It was a house of horrors. Seven children were rescued that night.

"Go get the truck and make it fast. I'm burning this place to the ground before we leave." Jared barked. Billy ran off into the night. Jared left the room going back to John who wanted to know what was going on.

"It was a freaking kid farm here. There's seven of them locked up in cages. Nearly dead." Jared told him. He pulled out his radio and got a hold of the compound to fill them in on what was going on. "All hands will be needed. Get everyone up. We'll be coming soon. Prep the surgical room. John was stabbed." At that moment Billy pulled into driveway, he left it running so they could use the headlights. They lifted the garage door open for a direct route. John was loaded up front in the passenger side. All the children were loaded up in the back. They were both terrified and relieved. Pulling away from the house Jared did as he said he would. Using a Molotov cocktail, he watched it burn for a minute. Cheers from the healthy children were heard in the background. Their nightmare, their hell was over, and they knew it.

Pulling into the compound, all the adults and teenagers were in complete shock at what they saw. Helping to unload the fragile frames, tears were going all around. They would get them cleaned up with new clothes and some food. Once they were settled in and taken care of, the next day they would need to answer some questions.

42.

Everyone had been up all night getting the children settled in and taken care of. Dwayne had been working on Johns' shoulder for several hours. He had scored some morphine from his work before he left the final day. It was a good thing he did too. The knife had gone into the Subscapularis muscle. It looked to have missed all tendons, that was what Dwayne worried about. He had to make the wound slightly bigger, the knife was wedged in there good and deep. The point was sticking out of the back about a half inch. He would need to be very careful not to make it worse as he slowly removed it. John would need to be on bed rest for a bit and go through some type of physical therapy. But all they had was time now. It's not like they needed to be somewhere or had completely busy and crazy schedules. Getting it out and cleaning the wound, he would need stitches and antibiotics...and they had plenty of both.

Linda and Dylan's wife, Kim, had started talking to the kids. Asking where were their parents? How did they end up there? How many before them? It was a very emotional interview. Some clammed up and didn't want to talk about it. They were still in shock, but a few were able to give them details in which they would have a meeting about.

Later that day when the ladies were done, they informed James.

"Ok. Kim and Linda were able to get a few answers out of the victims", James started. It was time for business and not emotions. "Apparently, some of them lived in that community. They were kidnapped one family at a time. She would go in at night, kill the parents, sometimes in front of them, and haul them away and put them in a cage saving them for a later day, and eat the parents first. She would force feed them some of what she didn't finish to fatten them up. Basically, feeding the parents to their own kids. The scrawny kids we've seen were found outside the area and brought in whenever she went out. They were alone out there and thought they could trust her. According to the ones that lived there, they all knew her. She was at their parties, baked cookies, entertained the families at her house before all of this, the whole nine yards. Close friends with everyone until her belly started growling apparently. Then it all changed."

Every person in the room was in shock. So much evil in so little time. How could humans do this to others?

"It's my best guess that that one in the car crash had just been invited in, saw what was going on and escaped. But that's an educated guess" Jared chimed in.

It would take a while for it to sink in. They all knew life was changing and the world was cruel, but never imagined it could be this close to home. They all went their separate ways for the rest of the day. They would need to process it and decided on what to do with the seven children. They would probably end up staying with them for a bit. James would need to get on the line with Lexington and give a progress report. He would do that now, so it would be fresh in his mind.

"Lexington this is the Plan B compound, come in, over"

"This is Lexington, send your traffic, over."

James was unsure on how to handle this, so he would just say it straight out and what went down.

"Lexington, we came across a cannibal and freed seven children. Need you to take them in, over."

"They're not the first and they won't be the last. We can't take anyone in. Resources are too thin. over"

James was getting aggravated. How would they support seven more mouths? "I'll be there soon to speak with the mayor, over and out." He turned the radio off so he wouldn't get a response.

43.

Heading towards town so he could get confirmation from the mayor himself. The compound really couldn't support more people. Jared was driving,

James rode shotgun, Daisy and Pete were in the back. Weapons facing outwards like always. It was getting worse out.

They made it to the Lexington borders without any problems, the same guard was there and recognized them. Waving them in and pointing them to the right direction. Pulling close to the mayor's office, only James and Jared went in.

"I've heard about your recent encounter. Let's hear all the details," the mayor said enthusiastically. Jared gave all the details leaving none out. He wanted Joe to see how bad it really was. When he was done Joe leaned back in his chair, obviously thinking hard.

"Here's the thing. We can't take them in. We have nearly 2,000 to take care of. We are running on fumes until the crops come in." He wasn't lying either. It looked like they all had dropped several pounds since the last meeting.

"I understand that, but we can't either." James said sternly.

"Listen and listen good", The mayor stood up to make his point clear, "We are on the verge of a town siege from Thomasville. They have been threatening us and sending out scouts to probe our weak spots. I doubt you knew this, so we can move on."

"Thomasville? What do they want?" James asked.

"Everything" Joe said, "That coward former mayor took up shelter there and has sold us out. Instead of improving and rebuilding, they want to take what we've been working on and do Gods-knows-what with the people here. They are bigger. I believe around 27,000. I'd say they're probably down to 19,000 if they've had the same luck as the rest of us. They still out number us by thousands though."

"Ok, we'll keep them with us. What are you going to do about Thomasville?" Jared was curious.

"At the moment, it's still in the works so we are trying to work out a peace deal." Joe wasn't down yet. He just wanted to try the least bloody way first.

With that, James and Jared left. They had never really thought about entire cities and towns fighting each other. This was something to be concerned about. If it were to spill over to their neck of the woods, they would be overrun easily. It was terrifying to think about to say the least. All they could do is help in some way. Do some recon to help spot the enemy. Something like that. Direct combat would be harder unless they joined up with Lexington and their defense force. Would 600 fighters be enough? Would they send them out to fight or just defend the walls? How long could they hold out? How many fighters did Thomasville have? These were the questions on everyone's minds once they told the adults at the compound. It was all everyone could think about over the next few days. A constant burning in the back of their brains that a crushing defeat could come at any minute. They needed to do something but what? Why did this have to happen? They were perfectly fine in the compound and cut off from everyone. The answers would come soon enough whether they wanted them or not.

The days went on, two weeks had passed since they brought in the new members. They were integrating into the families easily enough. Getting food and medical attention had brought them back from the brink of death. Although, the emotional scars were still there and would never go away. John was out of his bandages and had been on watch more frequently. It was the easiest place for him until he was completely healed. The embarrassment of getting taken down by a deranged nut job woman was fading. The jokes would always be there. He could except that and would just roll with it until someone else did something equally bad and embarrassing to take the attention away from him.

Some of the crops were coming in. It would be nice to get some of the fresh vegetables they were used to. They had to be in the gardens everyday picking off the bugs that would damage them. It was hard work without the use of pesticides, but it was absolutely needed to insure the minimum amount would be lost. Warmer weather was rolling in, they started to miss the convenience of air conditioning. They would have to settle for natural breezes to help with the coming summer days.

No word from the mayor yet on what would be

required of them. He must've been a busy man with all those people looking to him. Jared could understand that. They were now forty-two strong and it seemed like a small town to him. They really didn't need much. The solar panels they acquired made things a lot better.

44.

Todd and Gloria walked around the compound. After being here for a while it was like home. But they still would prefer their real home back and all the stuff they had to leave behind.

"What do you think happened to all of our friends?" Todd asked innocently.

"I don't know. I'm sure they are fine." Gloria tries to reassure him. It didn't work as well as she'd hoped but it was something.

"Do you think they starved to death?" Todd wanted to talk about it more. He wanted to think that they made it. But he knew everyone thought his dad went overboard with the emergency planning. He'd heard the jokes. But who's laughing now?

"Maybe they were able to get to a good safe place like we have here." Gloria wanted this conversation to be over.

"Maybe" Todd said and walked away.

August, Sandy, and Vicky walked up behind her. They wanted her attention. She was the oldest, and to them the coolest around. Given the lack of other teens, it was obvious why. They've watched her get training with the older men around here. It was something they wanted to do, Gloria should train them in her spare time. That sounded fair enough. They wouldn't do any shooting, but they do everything else. Using sticks as fake guns and knives she would teach them whatever she could to help them be better off in the future. Self-defense for a female would be a priority from now on. She wasn't sure if the parents would approve but she could at least try. It would give them all something to do in their down time and keep boredom away for a bit.

45.

Jared was messing around with and old fan trying to hook it up and make it solar powered. This would make some of the days coming more bearable. Doing little side projects like this helped pass the time when nothing was really going on. It helped to occupy the mind as well. If it worked then awesome, if not then he could try something else. He still used the wet sock trick to make his water cooler to drink. It was a trick most people that deployed to the desert knew, put your water bottle in a wet sock and as it evaporated it cooled the water. Simple and effective.

Gwen came and sat beside of him. She just wanted to see how he was doing and what he'd been up to. He had been messing around in the prepper binder that had projects he could do. He did complete a few, the red clay pot in pot cooling system. Rather easy, get two clay pots, one smaller than the other and set inside of the bigger one, then pour sand into the outer ring in between the two and moist with water. The evaporation will draw the warm air out and cool inside the smaller one to help keep things cooled down. Keeping some of these around will help during the really hot days. He would go through and do all of the easy ones first, then ask for help on the bigger ones.

As he looked around, everyone was moving about. It wasn't always about work. They needed fun as well. The kids were running around playing some tag game. The adults were talking with each other. Laugher floated across the yards. It was nice to hear the sound of a good time. What would be the point of surviving if it was all serious and you couldn't enjoy life at times?

Pete walked over and sat down next to him as he was still fiddling around with the wires.

"Nice weather we're having." The standard greeting for most men.

"Yea, I hope it stays this way for a bit." Jared stopped what he was doing.

"I've got a book on biodiesel. Maybe we can try it sometime. Take that beast out for a change. Ram through some cars and bring back some more stuff we can use." Pete was enthusiastic about the thought. He really wanted to learn how to drive it and ram into cars.

"Where are we going to get the right chemicals?"

Jared was intrigued. They had all thought about it, but no one had any experience. The pictures in the book didn't make it seem that hard.

"A lot of these wouldn't have been taken. People probably just over looked them while they were getting the other stuff. Can't be that hard to locate." Pete would start locating places he'd thought the chemicals would be at. They would need to make setup like the one in the book to get it all mixed together.

Martin walked over to join them. Tears still in eyes from whatever joke had been told. It must have been a good one. He swiped them away,

"Hey guys, what's up?"

"Just thinking about a few projects we can do around here. I see you're having a good day." Jared said with a smile.

"Can't complain. Couldn't sleep earlier. Watch is going to suck later." Martin said.

"Let's just be glad it's quiet for now. I really don't want another adventure like a few weeks ago." Jared said referring to the cannibal lady.

"Odds are we're bound to run into more of those sickos." Pete was sure of it.

"Any word from the Mayor?" Martin asked.

"Nah, but I guess I can get on the horn with him."

Jared offered.

"Screw that." Pete jumped up. "Let's take the War Pig out and hit some of these spots for the diesel ingredients on our way to town."

Jared thought it over for a moment then agreed. He would like to know what's going on in town.

The three geared up and got the War Pig ready. They let James know what they were doing and where'd they be. Keeping in contact with the compound was essential.

"Headed into town. Need anything?" Jared asked sarcastically.

"Is it necessary to leave?" James asked.

"Yup. Going to see what's going on into town and locate some stuff to make biodiesel. It's much needed around here."

"Ok. Be safe and check in." James waved him away, so they could head out.

46.

They took a different route to town. Didn't want to keep going the same way several times in a row to get to Main Street. That was just asking for an ambush. Jared drove, Pete was riding shotgun, and Martin was in the bed of the truck, so he could cover their rear. This truck would be a prized haul if someone could catch them. They would take South Main street again once they got there. It would allow them to stop at several businesses on the way home to search for the ingredients. They would need Lye, cooking oil from restaurants (used or new), and methanol. These are what they wanted after they met with the mayor. Same old thing going towards town, trash and dirty people were out in force now. The warm weather must have gotten them to come out of whatever hidey hole they were in. Jared wondered how these people were making it. No doubt the local wildlife took a major hit that would take years to come back from. Just as he said that a rugged looking woman held out her arm, a rat dangled from its tail, dead. Either she was offering it, or she was crazy. Best not to chance it and they never slowed down until they reached the gate.

A different set of guards were on watch, but there had been a quick entry list made and Jared was on it. "I guess I'm kind of important" He said to the guard.

"Just shut up and go inside" The man was in no mood for small talk.

With the gate opened, they drove inside. It was looking better and better inside these walls. Projects were getting done and the people seemed happier for now. Eyes all over the town shifted towards the War Pig as they drove towards the office.

"I'll go inside. You two stay here." Jared parked and went inside.

Joe was talking on a satellite phone and he was not

happy.

"I need someone from your office to get involved. Thomasville will not leave us alone and it could start and all out city war. Now, I've been trying everything I can to get them to stop but it's not working." Joe stopped talking and was listening. Jared couldn't hear the other person, but it did not sound good. "Yes, yes, yes...I know that. But...." He was cut off. The phone went silent. The other side had hung up.

He tossed the phone onto the desk not caring if he broke it. With the lack of results, he was getting, it might as well have been a paper weight. Looking at Jared he assumed he had heard it all.

"They've sent a truck of fuel and food to Lexington and Thomasville to help ease the tensions a few days ago. Even with that shipment, they are not backing down. They want it all. I had expected this from Salisbury but not Thomasville. Salisbury has minded their own business for now." Joe was exhausted. This was taking too much of a toll on him. He sat down and leaned back in his chair. "What can I do for you?"

"I've heard all the information I needed to know. Raleigh isn't going to step in. Are they?" Jared asked.

"No. It gets worse as well. Most of the aid from the other countries are winding down. They say they'll need it for the War effort soon." Joe rubbed his face. "Also, no power plants and transformers are being built. China and Russia have both agreed not to build any and

150

ship to us. China obviously because they helped do this. But now they've convinced Russia to step back and watch. They want us to fail. We can build a few here. But the amount needed will take decades at this rate."

"Holy shit" Jared was stunned. "So, this is life now? What war effort?"

"From the grapevine, if it's true or not, the countries that did this are mounting one hell of a front in Europe and the Middle East. I don't know what they plan on doing. But America is too weak and damaged to fight another war." Joe was in awe. He'd never thought he'd live to see this day.

Jared pulled a seat close to the desk, "What do we do now?"

"Once again, it's only going to get worse. We've hit rock bottom and that bottom just gave way and we're falling even deeper. Instead of working with each other, people just take from one another. It's sickening." Joe was furious with the state capitol.

Jared stood up, this was his cue to leave. Joe had a lot going on and didn't need him to bother him. Getting back to the truck, a small crowd had come to look at it. It wasn't something people saw every day. It was an attention getter, not exactly gray man material but you never know when you'll need to plow through something these days.

"Time to go. Load up" Jared raised his arm and

did a circular motion in the air. The signal for "mount up". They could hear a few shouts but were unrecognizable under the engine. They started to drive off when someone jumped onto the driver's side door and began to jerk at Jared's gear. The door was locked so the man couldn't open the armored door, he could only reach in the rolled down window. Jared hit the brakes and came to a complete stop to try and shake him off, but it didn't work. There were too many places to grab onto for support. The man yells as he pulled Jared as hard as he could,

"GET OUT OF THE TRUCK!!".

It was close to his face, so he could hear him clearly. Jared tried to fight him off by hitting his hands. It didn't work. Another person jumped onto the passenger side and began to fight with Pete. Martin was in the back with several people trying to get into the bed as well.

"GO, GO, GO" Pete yelled as he punches the person several times. More people were surrounding them, trying to get on. Jared hit the pedal to the floor. The massive truck lurched forward. The ones in the front scattered, all but one. The truck bounced as it ran over whoever was dumb enough to get in the way. It was time to get the rest off.

"FIRE ABOVE THEIR HEADS", Jared shouted as he pulled a pistol from the conceal holster that was mounted. He fired a shot that just missed the man's head, he jumped off immediately. Pete reared back and rammed the butt of his rifle directly into the man's nose.

Blood exploded out as he fell off. Gun fire came from the rear as Martin shot several people trying to pull him over. Bodies fell to the ground as the rest scattered away from the truck. This was not a 'Gun Free zone' so many of the citizens still carried a weapon. Someone on the driver's side raised a shotgun and fired into the driver side door not knowing it had armor. The 3/8-inch-thick AR500 plate easily defeated the slug. It broke apart as it ricocheted off and tore into a bystander. Jared didn't look back as he barreled away and headed for the gate. Mayor Joe had been watching from windows, there was nothing he could do now. It was mob rule down there.

"Call the gate and let them through" He told the former military guard that stayed with him at all times. In the aftermath, one had been run over and laid smashed in the street, four were shot in the back of the truck, they fell as they were shot and the other was dumped overboard as they rode away, one broken nose from the butt stroke to the face, and one injured from ricochets. Five dead and two injured. That was Five less mouths to feed from their own stupidity. It sounded cruel to say it like that, but that was the way of the world now.

The gate was already open by the time they got there. They would've rammed it if it wasn't. This was a scary lesson to be learned the hard way. Next time, it would be shoot first, then ask questions later. What if the guy had stabbed him or pulled a gun? Too many what-if scenarios for non-lethal actions anymore.

47.

Leaving the Lexington walls, it was time to look for the biodiesel ingredients. They were all on edge from the attempted hijacking, but the mission was not complete. They still needed to look for what they needed. The first and easiest would be the cooking oil. They had a plastic 55-gallon drum barrel they could store it in if it wasn't already in a container. The closest business would be *Bojangles chicken and biscuits* heading back down South Main street. They would need to be extra careful doing this. One working and two lookouts. The oil bin was outside beside the dumpster, so it was easy to pull up next to. Jared stayed at the front of the truck and Martin stayed in the back, since it was Pete's idea he could do the nasty work of transferring it over. The hand pump they used would work. They would have to filter the food chunks out of it when they got back. The oil was thick from being used so it took some time. Several people were started to come around. The dead rat lady seemed to be the most interested. She moved closer still holding a rat. Her clothes her caked in filth. This life had hit her hard. Jared wondered what she did for a living before all of this. She eased forward even more. Jared wasn't going to take a chance.

"That's close enough lady." He didn't point his rifle just yet but was ready to. She moved closer still like his voice wasn't being heard.

"Don't do it. I said that's close enough." Jared aim his rifle. He didn't want to but from what just happened he really couldn't help it.

"Trade?" She said in a low rusty voice.

"What?" Jared asked. It was hard to hear her. It sounded like her voice had gone hoarse.

She held the rat out further, "Trade?"

"Ok, what do you need?" Jared's talking got the others attention. Pete was nearly done. Just another minute or two.

"Anything. Anything will do" She strained to get the words out.

"You keep the rat. I'll pass on that", He reached into the truck and pulled out an MRE and tossed it to her. She caught it and began to shuffle off. Suddenly, A man ran from where ever he was hiding and tackled her to the ground trying to wrestle the food away. Jared shouted and ran over. The man didn't let up and continued what he was doing. Jared wasn't about to jump on top of him. Instead, he gave a stiff right boot to the temple. The man didn't stop still. Jared had had enough. He could make the man leave but what would stop him from following her when they left and doing horrible things to her. Jared kneeled, stuck the rifle to the man's head and pulled trigger. The gun fire echoed off the buildings. The man fell over dead, blood and brains began to pool under him. The woman just got up and left like someone wasn't just killed on top of her. She must've seen some bad stuff these past few months for her to shake it off like that.

Pete and Martin stopped what they were doing and just stared at Jared. "Let's go. Times up here." He said and jumped in the truck. They did as they were told. The truck came to life and headed towards the next objective. Lye would be found at the plumbing distributor, it was used as a shower or sink drain cleaner. They were sure to have some. They could've gone back to Lanier's hardware but that was out of the question for today. Next would have to be the plumbing distributor just down the road. The actual name had slipped his mind, but he would know it when he saw it.

They pulled into the back of the store where deliveries were dropped off. This way he could back up to the dock and they could wheel the lye out on a cart. Making it easier and faster for everyone. Smarter not harder. They would just have one on watch outside. Jared would stay with the truck for a hasty escape if necessary. Pete and Martin would clear the building first, so no squatter would get the jump on them as they worked.

Moving inside and stacking on the doors for entry like they did during drills, they moved in. In the back of the store it was dark. Little windows at the top didn't let in much light. Flashlights lit up the area as they moved through, communicating the whole way. All the storage aisles were cleared. Stacking on the door that went up front where the customers would shop they moved smoothly into the next room clearing the rest of the building.

"Building clear" Pete said into the radio to let Jared know.

"Got it" Jared confirmed.

They looked everywhere they could, this place hasn't been touched except for vandals smashing windows and getting into the cash register. It was easy to find. But all they had were the small boxes for home use. Martin grabbed a cart and they loaded up what they could find. Satisfied for the moment they headed to the rear of the store to look for more that the management had stocked but not out front. Another buggy filled. Time to go. Each pushed a buggy right into the bed of the truck as planned.

"Two down and one to go", Pete said happily as they pulled out. The last would be a little more difficult to find, Methanol. They couldn't just order it online and any type of racing fuel was sure to be used up already. So, the next best thing would to be ethanol such as grain alcohol, but they would not want to waste corn or anything else to make alcohol just yet. So, that would leave *Heet: gas line antifreeze and water remover* that any and all auto parts stores would have. This would be a crude way to make the fuel, but beggars can't be choosers. This would be for the other smaller diesel vehicles at the compound. The War Pig would use motor oil until that finally dried up. But from the number of abandoned cars around, that wouldn't be an issue anytime soon. There were several auto parts stores around Lexington and Tyro, so this should be an easy job. This was one of the popular topics on the Apocalypse forums and chat rooms online as well as magazines and books.

They were able to get into both auto parts stores in Lexington, they contained a combination of sixty-three bottles. Most were the smaller individual use sizes, but a few were the bulk gallon types. They would be able to make about 100 gallons of the stuff. That would get them along for a little bit until they were able to find something else. Heading back to the compound they would begin setting everything up. It would be a basic and primitive setup, but they had plenty of time to perfect it.

"Before we head back, I'd like to drop by my house and see how it's holding up." Jared said to the others.

"Fine by us. Let's roll", Pete said loudly over the engine.

They headed towards his house enjoying the familiar scenery. The places that they had pasted countless times over the years. It all looked terrible now, but the memories were what made them smile. Getting closer to his *real* home, Jared was giddy with excitement. Like a young school boy heading home from school after a long day. The smile stopped as they got closer to where the house was. A pile of black and gray ash and a still standing chimney was all that was left. Someone had burnt his house to the ground. Jared killed the engine, so he could get out for a better look. He was in shock to find his home he had lived in for so many years in a pile that would fit into a small box truck.

"What the hell happened here?" Martin asked looking around.

Jared didn't say anything. He just walked into the ash pile and started moving it around with his boots. Pete and Martin just stood back not saying anything. They may have been jokesters but even they knew when to keep their mouth shut. Jared just went around in circles looking for anything that used to be his. Nothing. Bed springs and nails was all that had survived the fire. He looked over towards his old neighbor. The windows were busted out and the doors had been kicked in. It was obvious he wasn't there...possibly not even alive.

"It's all gone", he said in a sad and depressed tone. "Years of work and dedication and it's all gone."

"I wonder what happened?" Pete finally spoke up.

"None of the other houses are burnt down so I believe I know exactly what happened. " Jared continued. "It was probably someone that knew about all of my preps and came by for them. When they saw I stuck to my word about not being here if something bad happened, they must've lost it and set it on fire."

"That'd be my best guess as well." Martin said. "The out building and chicken coop are gone too."

Jared didn't even pay attention to those, but he turned and saw he was right. They had been scorched to the ground. "A damn shame. They never took me seriously or my advice and decided to take it out on my home. I told them time and time again, not *if* but *when*, something bad will happen to be ready. And this is how they repay me."

They all headed back towards the truck. There was nothing more they could do there. It was just a pile of ash and metal. There truly was no going back now. Jared had tears in his eyes as he cranked the War Pig up and headed to his new home.

48.

After the excitement from the trip today, they all agreed it was nice to be home. Pulling through the gates was a breath of fresh air. Time to unload the new supplies then relax for a bit. They had been gone for nearly five hours. Doing the radio checks with James was standard procedures while away from home. He didn't go into detail over the radio, so he would need to fill everyone in when he got a chance. They would probably leave the War Pig here next time they went into town...if they ever decided to go back that is. They weren't exactly in a rush to go back anytime soon. Just stay out of the way unless it was absolutely necessary. No doubt they would be a target next time by the man that started it all and the families of the dead. It was self-defense and nothing else. Their consciences were clear. They did nothing wrong. Jared went to his room to lick his wounds. Martin and Pete filled James in on everything including the house part.

49.

Another week had passed without any more incidents happening. Constantly trying to improve their living conditions and make the new type of fuel was a full-time job. Chores, chores, and more chores. That was what TEOTWAWKI had brought on them. It could always be worse. Just looking anywhere outside of these walls was proof enough of that. If they were able to produce more than they could use or store, they would find another small community to trade with. Maybe even the city of Lexington if they played nice.

Jared continued his training with Todd and Gloria. They would need to know how to defend themselves in this harsh new world. Using emptied weapons, they would learn to maneuver around others and move like a team. One day it would be up to them to protect the compound or where ever they ended up. Moving from cover to cover, Jared showed them the basics. Gloria was a crack shot while perched somewhere but moving and still hitting the target was another ball game. They would use real ammo outside of the walls and away from home, somewhere like an abandoned housing complex. One day. Ammo wasn't exactly something you could just waste. Once it was gone, that was it. No more super stores or gun stores to run to when you got low. Using terrain and learning the difference between cover verses concealment. Sandbags are better than bricks, stay at least six inches off a wall when close to it because of ricochets and fragments. Don't stand in front of a door or walk in front of a window. Details like these that could make or break them. It was a lot to take in, repetition was the key. Practice, practice, and more practice was the only way to make it sink it and stay.

Once the other children were old enough they would be out there doing the same thing. Abby's kids would be next in line, he didn't know Gloria was already training them. Jared wasn't sure how their mom would take it but if he was a betting man, he would bet she would be fine with it. She would have to be. There was no telling how long this would last. Using a bow and arrow was Todd's favorite, he had to use one since a crossbow was too hard for him to cock. He likes the idea of being something like one of his favorite comic book characters who only used arrows. Also, he could always run and retrieve the arrows during practice. Since it was silent, they were able to do that kind of training a lot and inside the compound walls. Learning about wild edible plants was one that most of the kids could get into, even the rescued ones if they wanted to try it out. Setting up snares for the increasingly rare small animals, learning about dead fall traps as well as various fishing traps. It was a school of survival that needed to be passed on. All the knowledge that their ancestors knew that had been lost over the past several generations had to be relearned. Jared's small library of survival books was worth its weight in gold, just as he thought it would've been. He was glad to have them, so was everyone else. The other members of the crew were able to lend him some that he didn't have as well as teach classes. The one plant that was massive and grew in many places around Lexington was the used-to-be nuisance plant, Kudzu. The state had a problem with it, it was everywhere. Climbing, coiling, and strangling the wooded areas along highways and rural places alike. Now, it was a God send. Plentiful and easy to identify. Nearly all parts were edible except the vines. The leaves, buds, flowers, and roots. The roots had a few directions they could go so he would always refer to the edible books for how to prepare it.

Since the blackout started, more and more people started to realize it was edible. They were eating things they never thought they would have to. But if they wanted to survive, they would. Still many people had starved to death. They were hard-headed and had queasy stomachs. If it wasn't from a can or grocery store, they didn't eat it. If it didn't look like something they were used to, like the standard vegetables' carrots, lettuce, spinach, and the others found in stores, they left it alone. Their mistake and they would pay with their lives for it. There were also people dying from eating toxic look alike plants that they couldn't properly identify. It was a mess when someone thought they could just wing it, head to the woods and live off the land. Nature was a cruel teacher, she'll kill her students and not think twice about it.

50.

"Jared, the Mayor is on the radio for you", James

walked over to him. "It's only been a week since your last visit. You think he wants revenge?"

"Nah, if he wanted that he'd hit us already", Jared said as he cleaned his rifle. Keeping a well cleaned rifle was a must. Rust was the enemy.

"Didn't think he knew where we lived", James wondered.

"As far as I know he doesn't. That doesn't mean he couldn't find us. He has the man power that's for sure." Jared cleaned up the mess and reassembled his weapon. "Let's just go see."

They walked into the watch dog post where the radio was posted. It was there so they could monitor it around the clock. Might as well since they would always have a guard awake.

"Mayor Joe, how may I help you, over" Jared smiled as he clicked the mike on.

"Just wanted to let you know there is no hard feelings here about last week, over" Joe sounded sincere.

"I should hope not. It was self-defense. Over" Jared didn't want any more drama. He'd had enough.

"I let the public know I saw it all and gave them my opinion on the matter. Nearly all are good with it, some not so much but that's a given. Over" Joe was happy about his call. He believed it was the right thing to do.

"Ok thanks. Anything else" Over" Jared wanted it to be over.

"I waited a week, so everyone would be cooled off and level headed. If you have access to a radio, you may want to listen to it tonight at 8pm. A special broadcast coming from the new government-controlled news media with information has been scheduled. Over and out" Joe left it at that.

"A special broadcast? I'm intrigued" Jared said to James and the others on watch. He put the mic down and walked away. It would be a few more hours until the broadcast, he would want to make sure everyone was there and to have good reception.

The AM/FM emergency radio had a permanent spot in Jared's house. He was able to run an antenna wire up a pole that was mounted to side of the house that was supposed to be for a cable line. The extra-long improvised antenna would give better clarity for what he thought would be a very important announcement.

It was five minutes until 8pm and everyone was wondering what the broadcast would be about. Some speculated and hoped for a miracle such as the aid would continue instead of dwindling down like Joe had said. It could be the power stations were being worked on. Maybe it was news of World War 3 kicking off and our Allies were getting into the thick of it. It was all speculation. It could just be some suit wanting to get on the air and talk about coming together in this hour of need.

8pm and the radio came to life,

"*Good evening my fellow Americans*" Just hearing that part, Jared knew it was the president. It was how they always started. "*I hope this message finds you well and in good spirits. In this, our greatest hour of need, it's been nearly 5 months since our country was caught off guard and our electrical system came crashing down. I know it has been a challenge to get what you need. Our country has never seen a disaster like this ever in modern history. Yes, many are dead. Many are wounded. Many from their fellow Americans and the civil unrest that has followed. We must remind everyone that all laws are still in effect. My staff and I have been working around the clock to get this great nation back on its feet and moving forward. Desperate times call for desperate measures. Many of our Allies have scaled back their aid and support. It is no secret that the world is on the verge of another world war and they will need all they can get to supply their troops. The United Nations has been doing their best to deescalate the ongoing situation, but it doesn't look promising. We need to come together as a nation and rebuild so we can once again be the world's most powerful nation. It is estimated that nearly 25% of our population is dead or dying. We cannot allow this to continue. I didn't want to do this, but it has been a long time coming. To get this country back on its feet in the fastest way possible, those with skills that are familiar with electrical systems of any and every kind are to report to their respective state capitols for assignment. This is not optional and will be enforced. Martial law continues to stay in affect. Yes,* *this includes the suspension of the constitution and its amendments but only out of necessity. If you see a law enforcement personal, you must surrender your weapons for the safety of others. We cannot and will not have more avoidable death at the hands of the untrained civilian population. The fourth amendment as well. In order to keep folks safe, we'll need to search and seize whatever the country needs in order to help the collective as per **Executive Order 13603: The National Defense Resources Preparedness.** A new program will begin to roll out as we consolidate our forces and resources to bring this country back to its former glory. We understand that not all Americans have access to a radio and are unable to hear this, so we will task the locals to spread the word accordingly and comply with the coming changes. Thank you and goodnight."*

With that broadcast, even more confusion and questions flared up within the small community.

"What does this mean?" A frightened Gwen asked to no one in particular.

"Forced work camps I assume," Jared said. He wasn't sure but that's what it sounded like to him. "They will probably offer food, medical, and security and folks will voluntarily go. Some, like us, will not."

"Then what happens?" Daisy asked.

"Either comply or go with an armed resistance." James cut in.

"We've been doing great for nearly half a year. I think I'll take my chances here." Billy announced.

Walter sat in the back in complete silence. He was content here but was thinking about the current situation and the news he just heard. Would his family be better off going? Surely, the government had better resources than this ragtag group of people that *think* they know what to do. Sure, they were doing fine now, but what about when the good times ended...again? Would they be able to pull through? He doubted it.

"This could be a good thing, right?" Abby insisted. "Instead of people just sitting around and doing nothing they will start being productive."

"And what about the ones that know nothing on the subject matters they want? Will families be taken care of?" Walter finally spoke up. He was really thinking about it. This may be his ticket back to some sort of normalcy.

"Whelp, I believe I'm going to stay here" Dylan said speaking up for his family.

"I'm sure they'll have openings for ditch diggers and part haulers if you want to take your chances Walter." Jared directed towards him.

" I didn't like the way he said it would be enforced" Linda interjected. "What happens to those that refuse?"

"Either taken by force or shot probably. They will not want to show any weakness especially if there's a crowd around." Martin chimed in. He was an avid internet video watcher on most conspiracy theories. Except for the lizard people and flat earth society. Even he wasn't falling for those. "This country has fell apart at the seams. They cannot control those that are self-sufficient like we've become. They want you in debt and relying on them as much as possible, so they can have you do whatever they want."

"So, what now?" Gwen asked. Scared of the answers she'd get.

"Keep our heads down and watch it play out. You are free to go. This isn't a prison. Leave if you want." James told everyone. "As Billy said, I'm fine right here doing what we've been doing. I don't have any electrical experience, so they'd put me in some shit job probably."

With that being said, the meeting was done for the night. Everyone went their separate ways. Jared made his way up to the watch dogs to share what was said and the decisions of others. Some were on the line, others were sure where they wanted to be. Here.

51.

The next morning after everyone had a chance to sleep on it. They emerged from their homes like every other morning. It was time to get the day started. Jared walked outside to see a vehicle loaded up like someone was moving out. It was at Walters house. Jared walked over to see James was already inside talking to Walter and his wife.

"You can't be serious" James started.

"We believe it's the best chance to get back into a normal life" Jessica said. She actually believes things would go back to normal if they went and signed up for the nationalized labor force.

"I agree" Walter said. He didn't stop as he took more of their possessions through the front door. The little family car was packed down like a Grand Canyon touring mule.

"What do think they are going to do with an accountant and a house wife? Those aren't exactly relevant skills in these times." Jared started. "They want blue collar workers that are skilled laborers."

"We'll take are chances." That was all Jessica said as she grabbed their kid by the hand and guided him to the waiting car.

"We have a few gallons of gas to get us as far as possible. We'll trade for what we need" Walter offered his hand out for a shake. James took it. "Thank you for everything you've done for us."

"I wish you the best" he said as he shook Walter's hand. Walter got into the car and cranked it up. It struggled against the stale fuel, but it would work. James escorted them to the front gate, as he opened it he nodded his head. Just like that the family was out of sight. James closed the gate and walked back. He felt it in his gut they wouldn't make the two-hour drive to Raleigh. Two hours was the normal no traffic time. Who knows how long it will take them now. But ultimately it was their choice in the end. He just hoped they would be safe. Wishful thinking. Jessica couldn't keep her mouth shut and Walter was a weak and frail little man. It spelled trouble right from the get go.

James walked back to meet Jared after making sure the gate was firmly secured. The new cars they had put in after that crash were still in the same spots. Staggered so a vehicle couldn't get a speeding start and ram the gate. It worked just like it was supposed to last time.

"What do you think?" Jared asked.

"I think they are making a big mistake" James replied. "But there's nothing we can do about it. Let's spread the word that they left." They walked away doing small talk about what needed to get done. They would go through the recently vacant house to see if there was anything they could use and maybe spread out a little more.

Everyone took the news rather well. All the kids, tender hearted as they were, would miss their friend and the fun times they had together. It would feel a little emptier around here, but resources would go just a little bit further with three less people.

Getting the biodiesel station up and running wasn't as hard as they initially thought. The book was a great asset and proved to make things simpler as they read it over and over. The first batch wasn't a complete loss. It was a little harsh on the engines, but it would pass and get better the more they tweaked it. Most of everything they did had a learning curve. Having the books and reading about subjects, not training on it a lot before the blackout, was a different outcome. They really should've done more of these things beforehand. Oh well.

The distillery they had built for their water cleaning needs was doing great. They used it to save the water filters for their portable uses when out on scavenger missions. Doing it this way was the best way. Getting pure water from any type of nasty source was helpful. The stream they used was clear water but who knows what happened up stream. Doing it this way, they were able to get out any heavy metals, urine, poop particles, viruses, and bacteria. 100% clear, clean, pure water.

52.

"I've been thinking about what the president said, about it not being optional and being enforced", Jared was talking to Pete and John. John had since made a complete recovery from the knife attack. It was still sore at times or stiff in the morning but that would go away with time.

"What's on your mind?" John asked as they were

walking through the garden and picking bugs off the plants. It was a great treat for the chickens. The chicken feed had been exhausted so grass and bugs were on the menu from here on out.

"Our perimeter defense is seriously lacking. We have the cars to block other cars, a wall, and high-rise security. I don't think it will be enough" Jared was concerned about a lot of things and this one took priority at the moment.

"We can think of other means like booby traps. You know, trip wires and spike strips. My old man used to tell me stories from Vietnam. The things they came up with was a psychological mind game. It really did a number on the troops. Especially, when they actually hit one" Pete told him a few stories that his pop had told him over the years. Quite graphic and some good ideas.

"We could do the punji sticks or the Frankenstein" Jared said. He did remember a few improvised or field expedient weapons from his training. The Frankenstein was one nasty trick, a full spool of barbed wire with an explosive charge in the middle. It was said it could take out an entire platoon when hung from a tree. Shrapnel everywhere and in all directions. The punji sticks would be easy enough. Just make some pointy sticks and put them in a hole covered up. You could do some biological warfare and put feces on the sticks for added infections to the wounded. So many to do and no laws or lawyers to sue them if someone tripped them.

"We could also make something simple like boards with nails in them. Find the most obvious spot where an attacker would take cover, they would run and dive or slide then...bam...land on spiky board." Pete was getting too excited at the possibilities, but he did come up with some great ideas. It would definitely suck for the aggressors.

"Ok, sounds good. Let's put them into action" Jared let them use their imaginations to come up with simple yet effective traps and deterrence. It would keep them occupied. Plus, he was curious as to what they would come up with. Using a map of the compound that was hand drawn, they would know exactly where everything placed would be. It also showed the intersecting fields of fire from the pre-planned defense positions and where everyone would go.

They would place the traps when they went outside the walls to cut down trees for firewood. Chopping wood and hauling it in summer time was a hell of a task and the least favored by all. But it had to be done. Every house was responsible for their own firewood needs. This rule was setup, so some wouldn't try to skip out on that one chore everyone hated. If they tried or didn't do as much, then they would be cold come winter. Each house had a fire place, but it had been connected and made for natural gas. They had to cap off the supply outside and take out the lines in the fireplace. Simple task since there hasn't been gas flowing for months. Modern homes being built such as these weren't made for off the grid living so they would have to be altered and modified a bit for it to work as such. It wasn't hard or took long, just minor things here and there. However, not one had a wood burning stove for cooking. There was only one they found, and it was put in the vacant community house where they could all get together during the winter or stormy days to play board games or darts. Until they were able to find more for each house they would all end up cooking here unless they made their own contraption.

53.

Mid-July they assumed. There wasn't really a reason to keep up with the dates. Days come and go. They did know the heat was rising and the humidity was breath taking. Literally, after a rain fall and the sun came out the next day it could be hard to breath at times. Just looking out at the ground and seeing it become hazy from all the water evaporating. Sweat poured out from every place possible. Everyone was miserable, and misery brings short tempers and aggravation. Your clothes stuck to you from all the sweat. Night fall couldn't come soon enough. Even then it was hard to sleep. The mosquitoes would swarm and bite and suck your blood. Keeping the windows open and screens in helped some. But when it was time to be outside they came in force. They really would need to do something about them. Jared had a few cans of bug spray, but it wouldn't last long. A few days with everyone using them. This was summer in the Carolinas and they had another month and a half of it.

Their first round of crops had come in beautifully and they were able to harvest. The other ones would be coming in a few weeks since they planted them two weeks apart. There were plentiful amounts of all kinds of fruits and vegetables. They couldn't gorge themselves, Jared and the others would need to start dehydrating for the winter time. Having the solar panels would provide the power the dehydrators required and make it easier than doing the sun dehydrating. They found several more dehydrating units at a few different stores. People must've just skipped over them when going for the TVs and other electronics. Those were useless, but these would save them from the extreme hard times that come with winter. Other people's stupidity was their lucky day. Chopping wood and dehydrating food was the top of the list at the moment. While some where doing that, the others had to do a team effort of digging a root cellar the size of a small basement. None of the houses had one, just crawl spaces and that wouldn't be enough. They would use the wood and bricks from the unfinished house at the end of the street. It was nearly stripped clean and down to the studs. They would use every last bit of it. On the up side, that opened a good foundation where they could put another project one day. Maybe try out an aquaponics lab to start raising fish. A green house would need to be erected as well so they could continue to grow food all year around. The aquaponics had a few others curious about the idea. Once it was set up they would need to find some fish, if there was any left around here. One very bad thing about TEOTWAWKI was if they caught it, no matter the size or limit, they kept it. Stripping the lakes, rivers, and forest clean of wildlife.

The few smart critters would have to repopulate, Jared hoped they could and not go extinct.

54.

"Mayor Joe, it has been a few weeks since our last call. To what do I owe this pleasure?" James and Jared sat on watch duty when the radio went off and Joe wanted to have a chat.

"This is very important. I need you to keep eyes on your area to see if any strange activity is happening. Any large movement of people and vehicles. Thomasville is on the war path. Our intel has reported large amounts of gear and people are mobilizing. Possibly for an assault. They may want to flank us, so I need you to contact me if you do." Mayor Joe sounded like he was in full crisis mode.

"Uh, sure. But we are on the opposite side of them. Wouldn't that be an inconvenience for them to cross your turf then attack?" Jared asked.

"We've had a few skirmishes in the past few weeks. They've hit our scavenger parties and have been probing our walls for weak spots again. The food and fuel that Raleigh sent weeks ago did little to curve their plans. If fact, they made a deal with Raleigh, they'll send people in exchange for supplies." Joe sounded like a true leader. Planning and looking out for his people and their best possible interest. "We've tried to handle this peacefully and diplomatically, but it hasn't worked."

"You have a lot of trained people there. Can you not hold them off or defeat them?" James took the mic.

"All we want is to be left alone. They are rounding people up and shipping them off to the work camps in exchange for supplies and to be left out of the labor camp round ups. Damn Raleigh has taken advantage of their desperation and turned them into goons for hire. They've gone too far." Joe was getting frustrated and infuriated. Just talking about it made his head go hot.

"This sucks. It's wrong and they are desperate." Jared snatched the mic away. "We'll definitely be on the lookout and keep you informed."

"Thank you, over and out" Mayor Joe was gone.

Turning to each other they both had the same look of, "What in the hell is going on in the world today."

"So basically, Thomasville is no longer playing nice. What can we do to help?" Jared asked.

"Man, I don't know. This is bizarre. Like a movie or something crazy like that. How can they go around kidnapping people and trading them for food and gas?" James was bewildered. "But we need to do something that's for sure."

"Well shit, how do we break this to everyone?" Jared honestly didn't know.

"Like a band aid. Fast and painless" James was

right.

Once their relief showed up several hours later they filled them in. Now it was time to do the same to the others.

Once they were filled in, they really didn't know how to process this. How could they be so heartless and just send people away? What if they came under siege by hundreds of armed opponents? They would be slaughtered. So now what do they do? That was the number one question everyone was thinking.

"Ok. I'll start off" Jared said "The mayor wants us as an outpost. To keep an eye out. We can do that. We'll use the drone. Do fly overs and see what's out there. We'll stay close to here and keep it as low profile as possible."

"What if they follow the drone back?" Dwayne asked.

"We'll keep it low on the way out, go high when we get to a place we like, then back low for the return." James said.

"Will we be in any of the action?" Billy asked.

"Only in an absolute and unavoidable situation." Jared replied. All were good questions, and all were good answers. He was satisfied now. It was now time to plan their next moves. "We don't have the man power for an assault that size. If you want to go join Lexington's

179

defense force, then you can go. I won't stop you. I won't stop any of you. But we need every person here alive and well. It's your choice."

No one wanted to go.

55.

Everyone was on edge. The news they had just got from the good mayor, people being treated like cattle. Traded for food. They're sending anyone they can find that isn't a resident there and sending them off. They would let Raleigh decide what to do with them if they were not skilled labors that would be useful. What *would* happen to those that weren't useful? Would they send them back or let them loose? If only they had more information, that would be very helpful.

They made sure the drone had a full battery and Dylan's boy had been teaching them how to fly it. They weren't professionals, but they would learn fast...or crash. They didn't want to use the kid and his abilities just in case they saw something bad. No need to scar them for life even more than they already are.

The drone rose to the top of the trees and hovered. The video feed that went into the phone was crystal clear and ready for flight. Skimming the tree tops and heading north, which would be a likely avenue of approach from Thomasville, it flew five minutes out then went straight into the air for observation. The instrument panel on the controller said it was nearly 3,000 feet high. Turning in a slow 360 degree turn it was able to see a long way away. That did little good since it didn't have zoom in capabilities, so it came closer to the ground to get more detailed videos. Not seeing much, they were at the fifteen-minute mark, a little over half way through the battery. It flew north for another few minutes then into the air again. Still nothing that would cause an alarm. They could see a few cars moving about but nothing that would suggest an attack was imminent. It was time to return home and get a new battery. They had two spares, but the charge time was nearly an hour and a half when fully drained. Once it landed they changed batteries and sent it up again, this time to the east. Nothing to report.

"We'll need to get out and on the road if we want to get further out than just a few miles" Jared suggested. "Drive for a few miles then send it up. Plus, it'll keep onlookers from seeing it return to the compound."

"Ok, lets set up once all of the batteries are done charging." James said.

Nearly three hours later they were ready to go. They would take a smaller and more maneuverable diesel SUV that was less conspicuous than the War Pig. It still had enough force and speed to get away fast or push a vehicle out of the way if needed. They always went out in fours for security reasons. Dylan, Jared, Billy, and Martin were set to go. Full gear loaded up and a full tank of the new biodiesel. They headed east to get to the other side of Lexington, the side that Thomasville was located on and would drive north once they could.

Getting on Highway 64 they would go to exit 96 several miles away from the Lexington walls and get a better view of the area. Setting up at the top of the off ramp they set up a perimeter and began to get the drone ready. Once it was calibrated, up into the air it went. There wasn't a need to stay low since they were nowhere close to home. They would be able to get a better view and for clearer sightings, just a few hundred yards into the sky would be enough for now. Doing a 360 degree turn to start out with and making sure no one was advancing towards them, once they were satisfied the drone headed up the interstate. Cars were pushed off to the side for the most part, an old blockade that looked to have been destroyed blocked a small portion of the road still. They may have been burnt out, but they still choked most of the road. A one lane path had been made as the debris had been pushed to the side at one point. Continuing on they would head to the next off ramp that served as a rest stop. Plenty of room and it would make a good staging area for aggressors. Coming over the top they expected to see cars and people everywhere but nothing was there. A few cars that looked to be out of gas and had been abandoned littered the area. Not enough for an attack or to be concerned about.

"I don't see anything" Dylan said as he scanned the area.

"Go a little further. The Vietnam Veterans memorial park is connected to this place. Follow the back-entrance road." Jared directed. Martin and Billy were on both sides of the SUV keeping watch. You can never be too careful in this new, harsh reality. The drone went over tree tops, from the distance it could be nearly silent apart from a low humming sound from the motor. At a few hundred yards it wouldn't be heard. Seen, but not heard. As it closed in on the new area, trees blocked the view until it was right over top of it. Then they saw them.

"Got something" Dylan said in surprised voice. Jared glanced at the screen to reveal what looked to be nearly 500 vehicles.

"Quick, screen shot it for proof." Jared spat. He wanted to get various angles to see what kind of equipment they had, personal numbers, etc...

"Got it. Going to maneuver around for better pictures." Dylan eased the controls as the drone moved around. A flurry of movement on the ground caught his attention. Many of the people began pointing towards the drone. "Uh oh. We've been spotted. Time to go." Before it could even move it started to spiral out of control and fell to the ground.

"Shit. I think it was shot down", Jared said.

"Double shit, my boy is gonna be pissed." Dylan replied.

"Load up. Time to get out of here before their scouts are out looking." Jared yelled for the other two to get in the SUV. "Lets head to Lexington and warn the mayor now."

56.

Making it to the northern walls they were let in and went to the mayor's office. Parking in the same spot as the last time where the confrontation had been, three stayed with the SUV as Jared went inside.

"I've got some intel for you." Jared waved the phone in his hand.

"Now's not a good time." Mayor Joe replied.

"It's big. A rallying point for Thomasville I believe." Jared convinced him.

"Ok, let's see it. It had better be good. We're getting reports of massive movement." Joe said.

Jared brought up the picture on the phone for him to see. "We were only able to get one picture before we were shot down."

"Shot down?" Joe asked.

"We were using a toy drone for recon. It was shot down. This is a picture from twenty minutes ago at the Vietnam veteran's memorial past exit 96. I've counted a little over three hundred vehicles." It was less than what he had estimated, but it was still a lot. "It seems there are quite a few school buses and box trucks in the mix. You're looking at probably at least 1,000 people if those buses are full."

"Oh. I see. Maybe the buses are for taking

prisoners back." Joe was being optimistic.

"I honestly hope so. That would drastically reduce the number of fighters. Maybe to 700 if we're lucky." Jared actually hoped the buses were empty for that reason.

"Your definition and my definition of lucky is vastly different." Joe studied the picture more. "So they know they're being watched? Now they will be on the move faster." Joe looked at the guard and ordered, "All personal to their post. This is not a drill. Prepare for immediate attack." The guard ran out of the room to follow his orders.

"Yea, sorry about that. We didn't expect them to actually be there in such force. We were just looking for any advanced scouting parties." Jared was truly sorry.

"You got us some good information. I'm grateful for that. Now you'll want to leave before we seal the gates." Joe nodded his head towards the door.

"Good luck" With that said Jared was out the door and headed for the truck.

The three were still at the SUV when Jared came out, "Lets go." He tried to talk over an air raid siren like from the old wars. Someone must have bought it as a conversation piece and collectable. It was being put to good use now. At 139 decimals, it would easily be heard within the small cut off city.

"What the hell is going on here?" Martin looked around as the city came to life and people were running everywhere and, in every direction, "I'll tell you on the move" Jared and the three others loaded up and sped towards the southern gate.

"City is going into full lock down. Joe thinks they'll attack sooner since they were spotted." Jared filled them in as they went as fast as they could towards home.

"Makes sense. The element of surprise is gone. Hit them fast before they can fully get their defenses ready." It was at that moment the first sounds of gun fire were heard in the distance.

57.

Pulling into their own gates they were noticeably not themselves. James noticed it immediately the second he made it to the SUV as it parked.

"What happened now?" James asked.

"We found where the Thomasville rallying point was. Over 300 vehicles. Cars, trucks, box trucks, and school buses." Jared filled James in on what Joe and himself thought the numbers were and the gun fire that they heard as they left.

"Compound meeting", James informed everyone.

58.

The first vehicles to confront the northern city gates were just one final test to see what their reaction would be before it drove off. A small car returned with a white flag hanging from a tall stick as the passenger held it high through the sun roof. It slowly moved forward not wanting to draw more bullets. It stopped, and both the driver and the passenger exited the car. Neither were armed that the guards could see. The driver did however have his right arm in a sling like he'd been injured recently. They were only a few yards from the gate. The driver spoke in a loud and clear voice,

"We are here to talk terms. We want to speak with your leader."

The wall had nearly thirty guards, they all stared at the woman in the middle.

"He'll be here momentarily. No sudden moves" The woman called out. She was commander of the day guards and formerly a State Trooper Captain. Within a few minutes, the gates opened, and Mayor Joe walked out with a small security detail.

"I'm Mayor Joe, what can I do for you?" Joe held his hand out in a friendly gesture.

"Your unconditional surrender." The messenger said.

"Not going to happen." Joe replied.

"Your unconditional surrender" The messenger

repeated himself.

"Again, not going to happen. Anything else?" Joe asked confidently.

"Nope", The two men turned to leave. As they got into the car to leave and Joe was still outside of the gates, the driver blew the horn. It must've been a signal because a single bullet struck Mayor Joe in the middle of his forehead. An instant kill. The car sped forward and into the security detail running over the former mayor's body that just hit the ground. Gun fire erupted into the car as it tried to block the gates from closing. More gun fire came from several cars that were speeding forward at an attempt to get inside. The messenger's car did its job and blocked the car that was acting like a gate door from returning to its original closing spot. With men and women trying to push it closed the next vehicles punched through the gate and knocking it aside along with the dead messengers' car and sending the gate pushers violently to the ground. On the inside of the walls an armored Humvee sat silent until it had targets in sight, once they were in sight the .50 caliber machine gun opened up obliterating the three hostile cars and their occupants. The two 240 golf machine guns that shot 7.62mm bullets, that had been mounted and maintained by the guardsmen at the top of the walls, opened fire as more cars and trucks came around the corners at top speed. The rest of the guards continued to fire but were unable to stop many of the attackers. They were just too fast and too many. Superior numbers made it possible to make it in.

Enemy scouts on the roof tops directed the assaulting vehicles to the armored Humvee. It was the biggest threat and needed to be taken down. Punching through the gate they went straight for the military vehicle. It was able to kill a few but overwhelming numbers got the best of it as they rammed it, turning it over and onto its drivers' side. Enemy snipers emerged from the roof tops to kill as many as they could so the cars could get through faster and unopposed. Panic and confusion from an untested and barely operational civilian defense force swept through the ranks. More were on the building tops and engage the new enemy targets across the streets. It was a full-blown war on Lexington Main street. Deafening gun fire was all around. The former state trooper Captain, whose name was April, had been in a shootout before the blackout. It didn't last long, and she came out on top. It was still more than most of the residents here. She kept a level head and started shouting orders,

"MAINTAIN SUPPRESSIVE FIRE"

"GET THOSE CARS AND BLOCK THE GATE OPENING"

"GET THAT HUMVEE FLIPPED BACK OVER".

It must've gotten her squad leaders attention. They began to bark orders as well, trying to hold off the invaders and repeal the attack.

They used several other vehicles to block the gate

openings to make it denser when hit and harder to move. More enemy cars came but were now doing drive by shootings to keep their heads down. The machine gun nest on top of the old court house was able to engage in most of the fighting. It had a high advantage and was able to reach most of the northern spots. This nest was key to repeal the enemy snipers on the roof tops and windows. It had the ability to burst through brick and make their cover crumble making it easier for the Lexington roof top shooters to engage as well.

The radio April carried erupted in screams of another assault, this time on the eastern walls that were just basically cars and plywood with 2x4 studs. It was to keep foot traffic out, so it didn't have a main gate. Just a small man-sized door for the guards to use. It had been breached with an explosive device, the enemy had troops pouring in through the opening. The guards were overwhelmed and defeated. One of Lexington's platoon sized reaction forces headed that way. They were able kill several as they came in. That seemed to stop the assault from that end. But several dozen had made it in the walls and continued to kill and dismantle other security points. Being inside and cut off, they were easily dispatched once the locals were able to get together and start relying on the training Joe had taught them. Being civilians with less than a few months training, veterans who were rusty from years of civilian life, they were able to fight back at least. Dead and wounded piled up on both sides.

From the northern gates, enemy combatants with

potato launchers acting as makeshift mortars loaded with soda can bombs launched them over the walls. Explosions and shrapnel flew in all directions killing and wounding.

"TARGET THOSE LAUNCHERS" April yelled into her radio. Snipers from the rooftops moved their aim and took them down. Some of the soda can bombs that had been lit, exploded as the launchers fell to the ground. This was an all-out assault. Even though all the attackers so far had been killed or wounded and captured, the assault continued. This was a determined foe. They must have had a lot at stake to lose this many people and want to continue.

Another wave came from the west side wall. This was a bigger explosion. The entire wall erupted in smoke and fire. Wood, metal, and body parts flew into the air.

"Jesus, what now?" April said in a huff.

A large force of two hundred people ran through smoke and fire shooting at everything they saw. The Lexington fighters scattered to regain their composure. The roof top snipers fired into the crowd killing as many as they could as well as the court house machine gun that was able to be moved to the other side of the building by the two-man crew. This gave the ground forces a chance to turn around at the next sandbag barricade that had been erected since Joe had first heard of the threats weeks ago. A few dozen shooters fired into the crowd mowing down many of them, but it wasn't enough. The enemies swarm assault did exactly what it was supposed to do. The whole "they can't kill us all" tactic had made it to the sandbags and close combat started. Guns, knives, ball bats, feet and fists were used. People even biting their opponents just to get an advantage on them. The mix was thick, so the roof top shooters couldn't do anything but watch and pick off a straggler here and there. Reinforcements from the south gate arrived and they were able to turn the tide of the fight. It was so brutal even intestines and other body parts were on the ground causing some to slip and trip. Machetes and meat cleavers made cutting off body parts easier. Blood and brains, dead and wounded laid sprawled on the road from sidewalk to sidewalk. It was over in a matter of minutes. Hundreds of lives gone just that quickly. A slaughter house right on the streets. Blood stains would be there for years to come.

With the Humvee right side up, the biggest machine gun they had was ready for action again. The southern wall hadn't been hit yet. April wondered why. Were they concerned about spreading too thin? Was the front assault to hard and they lost too many? Did they think it was going to be easy? The coward former mayor must've fed them some old information and didn't know Joe would train the locals to defend themselves.

Too many unanswered questions. Too many bodies laid in the streets. Blood ran into the gutters and filled the road. There was probably well over four hundred that were killed that day. It would take a while to separate the people of Lexington from the Thomasville combatants. The gun fire had died down, a few shots were heard, probably targeting the ones that turn tail and ran. They may have been desperate, but they weren't about to risk everything on a well defended area.

"This was an absolute shit show" Aprils now second in command told her as they picked up Joe's body and the fallen security detail outside of the gate.

"I know. We were all inexperienced. But we'll learn from this and make this place a fortress for next time someone tries to do this." She said holding back the tears.

A winding noise could be heard. They all looked around. The sound was getting closer. From around the corner a remote-controlled car headed their way. A guard aimed at the car,

"Wait" April said. "It's carrying something. Looks like a radio."

The r/c car speed towards them then stopped as it got close. She was right, it was a radio. As soon as she picked it up a voice came over,

"I want to speak to the man in charge." The voice said.

"He's dead. I'm in charge" April said with a lump in her throat. It would all hit her tonight. A tidal wave of emotions would slam her like never before.

"Have you had enough?" The voice said. It sounded like the old mayor's voice, but she couldn't be sure. April looked around at her people moving bodies.

Clearing them away so they could have a clear path if more fighting started.

"You've lost more than us best I can tell" April managed.

"True, but we have more people than you do. You can't hold out forever. Your defenses are down. Your people are tired and wounded and nearly defeated. I will send everyone I have just to prove a point" The voice antagonized her.

"We'll never give up just for you to send us off and trade us away." April was getting more emotional than she should have. "How many of your people are willing to die before they say it's not worth it?"

Radio silence.

The silence went on for several minutes. April was getting nervous. "Back inside. Get ready for another wave." They all moved at once still moving the bodies of their dead friends and their beloved fallen leader.

April used her radio to alert every post to do what they could to secure the now gaping walls. It would need to be fast and everyone would need to reload. Ammo runners, the ones not fully capable of actual fighting such as the too young, too old, or disabled, went into a frenzy. Using bicycles with attached carts, they had a variety of ammunition to take to the different posts, so they could reload when low. Makeshift barricades went up as fast as they could. More bodies were moved. The prisoners were moved into the police departments jail cells and secured. There wasn't many. They would be interrogated the first chance they got.

Radio silence still. The unknown was making April fidgety. She wasn't sure how many of her fighters she still had left, but she may be able to fend off another wave if they were lucky. Minutes went by and nothing came over the radio. She was hesitant to speak into it. Not wanting to instigate anything she just left it alone but keeping it close in case the attackers called again.

Over an hour had passed and still nothing. Then the radio crackled, "The assault is over. Command is dead." Then nothing else. They must've cut theirs off. She wouldn't trust this. It could be a diversionary tactic to get them to drop their guard. She ordered the ammo haulers to collect all the dropped weapons and ammo they found from both friendly and enemy forces and get them ready for battle. Once all the posts had been resupplied they would work out a new schedule. Keeping the ones that were supposed to be resting close by. They would need to start moving the bodies and body parts into a better location to identify the fallen Lexington warriors...and soon so the smell and diseases won't spread.

The sound of an engine heading towards the Northern wall could be heard before the diesel truck came into view. A brand-new F-350 Super duty truck rounded the corner of a building with another white flag sticking out of the passenger window. It looked as if someone just went to the car lot and rode off with one when no one was around. April was called over to access the situation. She decided they weren't going to go outside of the gates to be fooled again. A mistake that cost Joe his life. The truck came to a stop close to the walls. All posts were alerted. A man got out of the truck with a black trash bag in his left hand and held up the other hand to show he was unarmed.

"Far enough" April said. The man stopped without saying anything. "What do you want?"

"We are done. Thomasville has halted the assault on Lexington. Our citizens won't fight a hardened target any longer." The man said.

"What's in the bag?" April demanded.

"A parting gift. A token of trust for a peace agreement" The man offered. "We'll be taking our business elsewhere." He dropped the bag, got in the truck and left. Once he was out of sight a guard was sent out to inspect the package. Wondering outside from the safety of the walls, the guard was noticeably scared. He was there watching when Joe took the shot to the head. He wasn't battle hardened. Just a few months ago before this all happened all he wanted to be was a professional gamer. Play video games all day and get paid for it. He was only nineteen and volunteered for this because he thought it would be like his favorite games *Call of Duty* or *Battlefield.* Was it too late to take back the oath to the Lexington defenses? Probably. Where would he go if he did? He finally reached the bag and lifted it up for the rest to see and started walking back.

"Open it out there" April commanded. She wasn't sure if it was a trap or not and wouldn't risk bringing it inside the walls. It could be some sort of explosive device. Looking confused he just stopped and gave her a look.

"I want to be inside there" He said pointing back at the gate.

"You will once you make sure the bag is safe" She replied. Hesitantly, he untwisted the bag and opened it. Looking inside, his face drained of all color and went completely white, then he passed out and dropped the bag. The bag fell and out roll two severed heads. The coward former Lexington mayors head and the Thomasville mayors head. Both rolled towards the side of the road where it sloped to allow rain to easily flow into the drains. Coming to a final stop, their eyes where still open and mouth contorted into a shocked expression. Their deaths must've been a complete shock to them. The people must've had enough from the losses they endured and said, "No more". Someone close to them decided to put an end to the bloodshed and take the fight somewhere else.

59.

Inside of Billy's house at the compound, the crew was going over what they thought was going on. They could only guess and imagine what happened as they were leaving. Getting eyes on would be the best thing to do. They would try the radio first to see if they could get some answers from Joe. As they sat there contemplating and discussing what was next, Gloria burst through the doors with tears in her eyes and crying loudly. Jared rushed over to see what was going on.

"L...L... Lexington is being attacked" She was barely able to get the words out. She was an emotional wreck.

"What?" Jared asked. "How do you know?"

"It's all...", a tightening of her throat and a short intake of breath was all she could manage at the moment. The others surrounded her wanting to know more.

"Give her some space" Jared said as he motioned for them to move backwards a few steps. "She was on watch, go see what the other person up there knows." He couldn't remember who she was paired with at the moment.

"Right" and out the door Billy went.

Jared did his best to try and calm her down, but she was mumbling incoherent words through her hands and choked on her sobs. "It's ok. Try to calm down and tell me what happened."

"It's...it's all over the radio" She said all that she could muster. It was too much for her.

A few minutes later, Billy returned with the

portable ham radio. Voices were screaming, it sounded like some were crying. It was hard to understand at times, but it was understandable once they realized what was going on. The posts had to communicate with ham radios instead of the regular 2-way walkie talkies, so they could be powered more efficiently with small solar panels and car batteries. Nearly all the small AA and AAA batteries in town were drained except for the few rechargeable that were floating around. Lexington was being overran by Thomasville forces and all they could do it listen. Gearing up and running straight into a fight would be completely reckless and suicidal. Both sides would end up shooting at them just from the shear confusion. No, they would have to wait and see how it would turn out. Lexington had a good standing defense force and should be able to hold their own against an assault. Gloria had to be escorted home. It was all too much for her to hear that her hometown was under siege. It was just crazy to think about even in these hard times. Daisy was up there alone so they would need to send someone else up there with her. Martin volunteered since his watch was next. He left to retrieve his gear.

It wasn't long until it was all over. It all happened in less than an hour. Word of Joe's death spread after the smoke had cleared. Jared took it the hardest. He was the one that talked with him the most and was able to get everything smoothed out and come to be an ally. He would miss him and his leadership. It sounded like this new person, April, kind of knew what she was doing. She stepped up when no one else could. The shocker to end the worst day they've ever had was the severed heads of two elected officials. It was all just so surreal. They didn't know what else to do so they just went their separate ways for the rest of the day.

60.

The next morning it all seemed like a bad dream. Something like this happening in modern day America. They all knew it wasn't some twisted plot their minds had made up. Jared couldn't sleep so he stayed near the radio the rest of the night. By the time the sun came up there was no real news to spread. They were still separating the bodies and finding the severed limbs to the rightful owners. The ones doing the cleaning were crying, gagging, and plenty of vomit was getting into the mix as they did their best to drag the bodies away. They would load the known enemies into the back of trucks and take them to the already over flowing cemetery to burn. Keeping the birds and other wildlife away was nearly impossible at night. But it did present an opportunity for some hungry hunters that didn't care what the animals feasted on, they would still eat the animals. An iron stomach was a new must during in this new era.

The next big challenge was proper medical care for the injured. Top of the line doctors and medicine were no more. Now it was time to use what was on hand, which wasn't much, as well as turning to old fashion medicinal plants and herbs. The death rate would be high simply from shock and blood loss. That didn't even include infections from the wounds, improperly sanitized medical instruments, and just plain nasty stuff floating in the air. They had a small hospital, or what was simply more of a nurse's station, in the former civics center that hosted plays at one time. It was manned by a few doctors that had left the hospital once the medical supplies and the generator had exhausted its fuel reserves, or who had retired in the recent years, several nurses that managed to survive, and a few veterinarian technicians that lived in the city. It was a rag tag team of medical experts with a wide variety of experiences, but it was working to keep them alive. Amputations were ongoing, limbs that were beyond saving had to be cut off. No morphine or any other type of pain killers were available. If the patient was lucky, they would pass out from the pain. Most however, did not. It took an entire team to hold them down while others used saw blades from the local hardware store, boiled for sanitation, to saw through the bones. They were using techniques from a century ago, cut off the circulation and have them bite down on something other than their tongue.

The smell of dead flesh and clotting blood had brought in another nuisance, flies. That was until an old retired doctor stepped in and told them about *maggot* wound healing. It had been used by Napoleons surgeons during his wars as well as during observations from the American civil war, World War 1 and World War 2. It had made a comeback in the 1980s as antibiotic resistant bacteria started appearing and approved by the FDA in 2004 for chronic or non-healing wounds. Although, the maggots of modern medicine were sterile and raised in sanitary conditions, they did not have this luxury and would need to do it the old fashion way. Finding maggots and cleaning them off the best they could, they put them in a cheesecloth and set them on the infected wounds like a tea bag. The fine cloth would allow the maggots to eat the dead flesh but not escape. It was primitive but had been proven to work in the past. With luck on their side, they would be able to save lives from the deadly infections without the much-needed antibiotics. Some were hesitant to use it at first then quickly realized they didn't really have any better options. So far Lexington's wounded numbered seventy-eight and the dead from battle stood at fifty-three with more succumbing to the wounds with each passing hour. Even with the medical staff and volunteers helping it only made a small difference. Only time will tell who lives past the next few weeks.

With so much happening with the recent attack, Lexington had a mixture of moods. Grieving and sadness for the dead and wounded, then there was the cheerful, grateful, and confident side from repealing a larger force from taking them all prisoner and living another day. The ones that were able to move around were in a rush to refortify the city walls the best they could. They pushed themselves hard, some so hard that they passed out from exhaustion and hunger. Truly only the strongest would survive this test.

61.

Over the next week, fourteen more wounded had died. Some infections were just too much to handle.

Others however, were able to be saved thanks to the primitive health care. There would be stories and drunken comparison for years to come of who had the worst and most painful procedure done and live to tell the tales. Getting a hand or an arm and even a leg cut off was bad enough, but the stories from those getting stomach surgeries and bullets pulled from necks and backs would be top of the list as well. One man even had to get his guts pushed back inside of him from when one of the soda can bombs landed at his feet. Laying there on the table, cut open but in shock from the nerve damage, this tough bastard lived another six months before he finally died from obvious complications. Stubborn to say the least. Getting shot was painful, getting it dug into, cut more, and pried around was just insult to injury and added to the pain.

62.

According to his watch that he had found with a date window built in, it was now 10 months into the blackout with no end in sight. Even though the US government had started taking people against their will or the ones that voluntarily went, parts to rebuild the electrical plants just weren't being build fast or efficient enough to make a difference anywhere near Jared and his new family. A lot of the materials needed use to come from the same countries that did this to begin with, so there was no chance of them sending relief.

A news report from last week had confirmed it and gave the new estimated deaths... nearly 100 million have died. Almost a third of the country has died from starvation, civil unrest such as towns fighting, people just killing to survive, and every medical sickness that would plague a downed society. It still wasn't over, and more deaths would come. It had brought America to its knees in just *one* day. Being so dependent on electricity we didn't stand a chance without it.

The world was now into the third month of World War 3 with Amcrican allies barely maintaining ground. They were all that stood in between America and a full-scale invasion. With America out of the fight and just standing on the side lines unable to provide troops or aid for offenses, no nuclear weapons had been fired...*yet.*

Made in the USA
Columbia, SC
05 November 2018